POLITICS IS
murder

An Iowa Mystery

Edited by Barbara Lounsberry

Commissioned by Public Radio KUNI

POLITICS IS Murder:
An Iowa Mystery

Barbara Lounsberry, Editor

Joe Sharpnack, Illustrator

Amy Roach, Designer

Gregory Shanley, Project Director

Jons Olsson, Project Finance/Marketing Director

ISBN 0-9662041-3-1

Published by Public Radio KUNI

University of Northern Iowa

Cedar Falls, Iowa 50613-0359

Politics is the
best show in America.

WILL ROGERS

contents

Foreword

"Politics makes strange bedfellows" as the old saying goes, and the mystery novel you are about to read presents you with the strangest, most colorful collection of candidates for governor Iowa has never produced.

16,000 Suspects: A RAGBRAI Mystery and *Time and Chance*, our who-dunit with a Mississippi Riverboat gambling scenario, have proven so popular that in the spring of this year, KUNI decided to embark on a third mystery novel, this time involving politics. *Politics is Murder* is set in the year leading up to the 2002 Iowa governor's election. As with KUNI's 1999 RAGBRAI murder mystery, the candidates criss-cross the state—from Lake Okoboji to Backbone State Park and from the Bix Festival to New Melleray Abby—dodging bullets all the way.

As with our previous serial novels, we contacted 18 Iowa writers and asked each to craft one of the novel's chapters. We have found that serial mystery novels offer readers double pleasure: the pleasure of the unfolding mystery itself, and the added pleasure of savoring the distinctive gifts of each writer. I was concerned we might be running low on new Iowa writers for the project, but that turned out to be far from the truth. In fact, many of the writers from our first two mysteries recommended other writers. Wendi Lee of Davenport was especially helpful in this regard. The truth is Iowa produces writers in the same abundance as it produces good citizens.

Once again you will be reading a novel written totally via email. The authors never met face to face, and likely will not until our book signing parties. The volume was written in the 18 weeks from April to August 2000. The authors were each given just one week to craft their chapters. When Friday rolled around, a completed chapter was emailed to UNI English Professor Barbara Lounsberry, who edited the chapter and then sent it on to Amy Roach, our talented designer and compositor, with copies to the other authors. Testament to the professionalism of these writers is the fact that every deadline was met and the level of collaboration was high. As with *16,000 Suspects*, we only gave our writers two pieces of information: who did it and why. All the rest—the colorful characters, settings, and plot twists— came from the writers' fertile imaginations. We were struck with how helpful the authors were to those writers following them. Often an author would tack on to his or her chapter "Notes to Future Writers" indicating red herrings that had been planted or key clues that could be used. As the book progressed, all of us began to take a keen interest, not only in who would survive and how the mystery would be resolved, but also in who would win the 2002 Iowa governor's race!

By the time you are reading this novel Jons Olsson, KUNI's Development Director for the last 22 years, will have retired. Jons has had a long and distinguished career, and has been essential to the success of KUNI's ventures in book publishing. This year Jons selected the *Politics is Murder* title and kept the project's budget in line. In truth, Jons has played a key role in the growth and success of KUNI/KHKE as a whole. He set the bar high for other employees by arriving early, being extraordinarily productive, and leaving late. His dedication, along with his sense of humor, will be greatly missed!

I would also like to thank Editor Barbara Lounsberry for another terrific job in helping create a novel by multiple authors. As editor of all three of our mystery novels, Barbara has developed some unique skills and has enhanced her already solid reputation as an editor and writer. As I told her over the summer, she is a pleasure to work with, always calm, organized, and creative. Designer Amy Roach has many of those same characteristics. Whenever a crisis developed in the novel's production phase, Amy was the first to say that everything would work out. Amy did another outstanding job with this volume. How many book covers offer a useful bookmark as well?

Joe Sharpnack donated his cover art. Our first two mystery novels'covers were spectacular, and Joe's work is in line with that fine tradition.

I would also like to thank my wife, Sonya Shanley, for editing assistance, and the University of Northern Iowa Graduate College for, once again, helping finance this endeavor. A final thanks to the entire KUNI staff. These books are enjoyable to put together, but it takes a great deal of hard work from the entire KUNI staff for them to be successfully marketed and distributed.

Now, with the heated presidential elections behind us, we hope you will be primed for *Politics is Murder.*

Greg Shanley
KUNI News Director
Book Project Director

1.

Debate at People's Park

By Mickey Zucker Reichert

A gentle April breeze wound through People's Park, carrying the scent of grilled hot dogs, hamburgers, and the sticky-sweet aroma of marshmallows. Zachary Carlton laid on a fluffy blue blanket by the lake, while his girlfriend, Shara Hemingly, sat staring out over the playgrounds. Shading his eyes from the sun, Carlton studied the streamers of kinky brown hair the wind floated from Hemingly's head. Arms muscled from field hockey lay casually at either side, her left hand pinning their Frisbee and her right resting lightly on his thigh. His memory filled in the details: wide-set green eyes, generous nose, sharp high cheekbones, and full-lips, usually splayed open in laughter. Large-boned and chested, she carried a bit too much weight in her hips and buttocks to meet most men's ideal, but her sense of humor and quick wit more than made up for what she lacked in physical attractiveness.

Carlton brushed back his own overlong, dark-blond hair, feeling lucky. His sophomore year at the University of Northern Iowa showed more promise than the previous one. He finally had the opportunity to take interesting, as well as required, classes. All of his professors seemed competent and reasonable, more quirky than boring but not eccentric enough to make every assignment an eye-rolling trial. And, despite all the college odds, Shara Hemingly still loved him

"So, who you voting for?" Hemingly's voice wafted into Carlton's reverie, becoming an integral part of it. He smiled, savoring the warm sun, the lazy Sunday in the park, the gentle joy of her presence.

Then, suddenly, Carlton realized Hemingly had asked him a real question. "Huh?" he said stupidly.

Hemingly turned to face her boyfriend, her brows raised playfully.

"What do you think we are, married? These are our courtship years, you creep. You're supposed to hang on my every—" she mocked a dreamy gesture "—melodious word."

Carlton propped himself on an elbow. "I'm pretty sure you're supposed to wait till marriage before calling me names." It amazed him how easily the "M"-word emerged from his mouth. He wondered what so many men feared about commitment. He would gladly spend an eternity with Shara Hemingly-Carlton.

Hemingly pretended to consider. "No, *creep's* all right. I'm just not supposed to eat more than a lettuce leaf in your presence. And I'm supposed to pretend I never go to the bathroom, burp, or fart."

"Ah," Carlton said with a smile, "now I get it."

"Good. You're trainable." Hemingly returned the grin broadly. "I like that in a man."

"Thank my mother." Carlton sat up, placing a lanky arm across Hemingly's left shoulder and back to her opposite hip. "Now, what was it you asked me?"

"The governor's primaries are coming up."

"Yeah." Carlton knew that. He was looking forward to his first vote. His father had always called it his patriotic duty and a privilege the majority of the world's population did not share. Carlton had found the description melodramatic until last year when the idea of finally getting a say in government policy actually became exciting. "The Republicans are coming here next week to debate."

"You want to go?"

"Sure." Carlton's politics ran to the left of center, but it seemed ludicrous to miss what seemed like a circus in the making. As if to make his first vote memorable, the sitting governor had decided not to run and, as a result, the field had become not only unusually large but remarkably peculiar as well. Though the lead Republican candidate, Robert "Bob" Blackwell, personified the standard white Protestant male, the others ran a strange gamut. There was the rising star, a sturdy, outspoken farm wife with sweeping ideas on agricultural policy, ethanol, and hog lots. Close on her heels came a charismatic priest, a mesmerizing speaker fresh from the monastery pushing an agenda of morality and high-riding values, including an end to violence. Carmelita Lopez, a Latino woman so dark-skinned she was repeatedly mistaken for African-American, had credible conservative ideas to help migrant workers as well as to provide tax cuts and balance the budget. The last, Jim Taverus, appeared the most extreme. A holocaust denier with rumored ties to the Ku Klux Klan, he seemed unlikely to win any support, especially in a college town.

Though tamer, the Democratic field included a professor, a confessed cross-dresser, an openly gay veteran, and a businessman accom-panied on the campaign trail by his dog, a boxer named Winston.

"Do you know where the debate's going to be?" he asked.

Hemingly blinked at Carlton, looking deep into his eyes. "You're kidding, right?"

Carlton blushed, feeling dense. "What? It's at my house or something?"

"It's here, Zach."

"Here?" He furrowed his brow. "Here at People's Park?"

"Yup."

"Wow." Carlton glanced around, at the swings squealing back and forth, the nearest shelter with its neat rows of picnic tables and benches, and the climbing structures swarmed with children. Three loosed dogs raced, yapped, and wrestled through the grass. A pair of overfed mallards paddled lazily in the center of the pond, ignoring hunks of bread littering the shore. "Here?" He repeated, then, worrying that he sounded stupid, he added, "Who'd have thunk it?"

"It's a cozy enough place." Hemingly snuggled into Carlton's armpit. "And there's plenty of room. They'll probably use the nearby Oster Regent Theatre."

"How appropriate."

"I've seen lots of parties here, some of them really loud. Even wedding receptions."

"Yeah." Carlton stroked Hemingly's well-padded hipbone. "But it's so open. What if it rains?"

Hemingly patted Carlton's leg, acknowledging his touch. "I'm sure they'll have some sort of awning to protect their royal heads. It's us who'll get wet."

"What about security?"

Hemingly snorted. "They'll have Secret Service or cops poking around here weeks in advance. Probably got some out there now, casing the joint."

"Casing the joint, huh?" Carlton rose, stretching his long legs, working out the kinks. "We've got their lingo. Now, shall we try and spot them?" He offered his arm.

Hemingly took his elbow with the grand delicacy of a queen. "Certainly."

They walked south, toward the nearest sand pit and its accompanying playground. Carlton found himself moving stiffly, constantly worried about banging into Hemingly. Finally, he lowered his arm, sliding his hand down her forearm until he caught her hand. Wrapping his fingers around hers, he continued more easily. He remembered striding proudly through the high school hallways, his arm winched around Nancy Conderoy's waist, and wondered now how he had managed to keep from tripping her.

"There," Hemingly said suddenly, inclining her head rightward.

"What?"

"That man. I'll bet he's Secret Service."

Carlton glanced in the indicated direction, uncertain which of several "Sunday fathers" she meant. "Isn't the Secret Service a federal agency? Wouldn't it be, I don't know, FBI or something?"

Hemingly turned Carlton a measuring stare. "As in *Federal* Bureau of Investigation?"

"Oh. Right." Carlton considered. "But I'm pretty sure the Secret Service is a branch of the Treasury. They only guard the President. So that's not right, either."

"State Secret Service, then."

"Never heard of that."

Hemingly's smile turned mischievous. "Wouldn't be secret if you had, now, would it?"

"S.S.S.," Carlton shortened, rubbing his chin. Sparse stubble rasped beneath his knuckle. "Sounds evil. How about we use State Secret Service Equivalent?"

"Fine." Hemingly shrugged, gaze still trained on the indicated man. "S.S.S.E., then." She slurred the acronym. "Sssseee—Hissy. And I still think he's one."

Carlton examined the men again. Everyone seemed to have at least one young child dragging him toward swings, slides, or calling "lookit lookit!" upside down from the top of some bar or pole. He picked the one who looked most military. "The big guy with the buzz cut?"

Hemingly rolled her pretty eyes. "Too obvious. I mean that one." She rocked her head toward the fathers again. "The skinny blond in the Chumbawumba tee shirt."

Swinging his gaze around, Carlton located the long-haired man, who also wore a cross on a chain and mirrored sunglasses. His shirt bore the dingy gray coloring that came with exposure to smoke. A tangle-haired girl of about four years raced suddenly to him, tugging on his tobacco-stained hand. "Oh, yea. He looks official."

"Isn't that the idea?" Hemingly said with a wink. "Blend in."

Tiring of the game, Carlton veered from the playground toward the bicycle path. "I don't think the Secret Service—sorry, the Hissy—bothers to 'blend in.' They're taking bullets anyway, right? Might as well stand out as much as possible."

"So," Hemingly asked again, "who are you voting for anyway?"

Carlton considered the question. He had already settled on the leading Democratic candidate, but he did not wish to start an argument. Hemingly called herself a "radical independent." Her favorite slogan was a facetious, fist-banging, "Moderation or else!" He knew she'd drop her vote on some impossibly small-time candidate like the Libertarian or the Natural Law or Green Party guy. One thing seemed certain, there was no dearth of contestants, "characters" as his roommate called them, for the 2002 Iowa governor's race. "Isn't the very hallmark of a democratic society the secret ballot?"

"Secret from the government." Hemingly swatted his arm with the backside of her free hand. "Not your girlfriend."

"I haven't made up my mind yet," Carlton lied. "I want to hear everyone's stance, make a wise choice for my first election. Someday, I want to tell my kids about each and every one, how I made my very first vote count, and how they should consider as carefully as I did."

"Oh my God!" Hemingly recoiled with a wordless, horrified noise. "You're ... you're ...." She adopted a breathy, Darth Vader tone. "... Luke, you're your father."

Carlton blushed. "I've been called worse." He added carefully,

"By you."

"You mean creep?"

"Yeah."

"Shame on me. I shouldn't dare eat with a mouth this dirty." Hemingly pursed her lips in a wry grimace, then raced toward the concrete construct on the southwest side of the park. Now painted with amateurish animal scenes, it had once served as the backdrop for a caged bear and a chimpanzee—or so Carlton's father claimed. Just to the south lay an abandoned prairie dog village; the animals had all tunneled out before he started kindergarten. Beyond the rocks lay a small, sparse forest, rarely frequented. The children preferred the colorful playgrounds, the ferris wheel, and the train to scaling rocks, and the parents chose the campsites near the grills, restrooms, and toys.

Playfully, Carlton dove for Hemingly's feet, sprawling them both to the ground. They rolled, laughing. Warmed by the contact, Carlton rose reluctantly.

"Race you to the woods," Hemingly teased.

Nothing could have pleased Carlton more. They had spent several half-hour sessions making out behind the wall, out of sight of the picnicking families, rollerbladers, and dog walkers.

Carlton measured his pace to keep Hemingly just ahead of him, though his long lean legs gave him the advantage. She moved like a lion, her muscled calves pumping easily toward the barrier. A moment later, they both arrived nearly simultaneously and barely winded. Hemingly shinnied up the painted concrete like a squirrel. Carlton caught handholds and hauled himself to the top.

For several moments they sat amid crushed weeds, sticks, and dirt that littered the top of the wall, swinging their legs like children and watching the play on the far side of the bike path. Dogs frolicked in the open field, tangling leashes that obeyed the letter of the law by their presence but were so lengthy they defied their owners' control. A mastiff towed its rollerblading mistress, galloping like a pony, its tongue lolling. A family of three children shook a plastic tablecloth over an outdoor table near one of the massive black-iron cooking grates. For a few hours, they could all forget that school started again tomorrow and just revel in the April sunshine.

Hemingly sprang suddenly behind the wall, dragging Carlton with her. They headed for their favorite kissing spot just beyond a ring of trees. The one time giggling children had interrupted them, they had found more than enough cover. They had watched the youngsters dance, bounce, and skitter along the concrete for a few minutes before racing back to the more ergonomic playthings. As far as the pair knew, the children had never seen them.

Suddenly, Shara Hemingly stopped dead. Her mouth gaped, and she loosed a high-pitched shriek. Heart pounding, sweat spangling his forehead, Carlton peered around his girlfriend. A man lay on the ground, very still. Dark patches stained his suit, as if someone had splashed him with wine, but the pool of scarlet around him belied that first impression. It was blood, dark, clotted, and evil smelling. Dark eyes stared sightlessly at the sky from features pale as wax. Startled, Carlton recognized that face.

It was the Republican front-runner, Bob Blackwell.

MICKEY ZUCKER REICHERT *is a pediatrician whose fifteen novels include* The Legend of Nightfall, The Unknown Soldier, Spirit Fox *(with Jennifer Wingert), and six internationally best-selling Renshai books. Mickey's most recent releases are* Flightless Falcon *and an omnibus paperback edition of* The Bifrost Guardians *series. Mickey's short fiction has appeared in dozens of anthologies. Her claims to fame: she has performed brain surgery and her parents really are rocket scientists.*

2.

The Police Investigation Begins

By Donald Harstad

Bill Haldeman, Special Agent, Iowa Division of Criminal Investigation, surveyed the area inside the yellow police tape that created a relatively quiet zone around the body of Robert Blackwell. Haldeman inhaled a deep breath, held it, and released the air in a long sigh. The scene was just too empty. Only Blackwell, supine in the grass, his arms spread wide. His suit coat was open, and the bloodstained white shirt was a much darker red than his red power tie.

His fly was unzipped, and his black framed glasses were askew, his mouth wide open. Haldeman turned to his partner, Michelle Dean. "What do you think, Mick?"

She shrugged. "Maybe he couldn't find the public restroom? No other reason to be this far from the beaten path. Sure looks surprised, doesn't he?"

Haldeman grinned. "Sure does."

They were waiting to actually touch the body until the Medical Examiner arrived. Michelle snapped three or four more shots with her 35-millimeter camera. Preserving the scene. Then she turned and took a half dozen photos as she panned the onlookers. Preserving that scene, as well. They'd go over the prints later, and see just how many of the faces in the gathering crowd could be identified. Haldeman gestured toward the young couple by the ambulance who were staring at them. "They're the ones who found him, huh?"

Michelle had been the first agent on the scene. "Yeah." She inserted a new roll of film into her camera, closed it, and labeled the container for the previous roll. "Just sort of wandered off to do a little sensitivity exercise in their favorite spot. The girl nearly stepped on him, I guess."

"They didn't hear anything?"

"No." She adjusted the camera strap. "They were just over there," she said, pointing to the cement wall. "They said they had been there for a while, and then came directly over here. They ran, I guess. Didn't see him go by, didn't hear anything unusual."

"He hasn't been here too long," said Haldeman. Another problem. No sound of a gunshot. "Somebody should have heard something."

"Silencer?"

"Either that, or a hell of a distance from here." He shrugged. "Anxious to see if we have an exit wound." With a long shot, the velocity of the projectile fell off, and there was a greater chance that the bullet remained in the body. Evidence.

"Officer, officer!" Both Haldeman and Dean looked up as a short, thin man in a suit was halted by a uniformed cop just outside the tape barrier. "Officer, I'm with the Blackwell campaign team! I have to talk with you!"

The agents walked to the tape. "And you are?" said Haldeman.

"Homer McGruder. Campaign manager."

With that, the thin man produced a business card. "We have to talk in confidence," he said as he handed the card to Haldeman. He lowered his voice. "There's something you need to know."

Opportunities seldom knock louder than that. Haldeman gestured the uniformed officer to back away, and he and Dean ducked under the tape to talk "in confidence" outside the crime scene. Haldeman noticed the smaller man's eyes dart toward Dean's v-necked blouse as she bent over to slip under the crime scene tape. It was a bad first impression to make with the agent.

"What can you tell us? I'm Special Agent Michelle Dean, and this is Special Agent William Haldeman. DCI."

"He's dead, isn't he?" asked McGruder. Dean turned around. From this angle about all you could see of Robert "Bob" Blackwell was from the hips on down. He looked pretty well undisturbed, with his polished brown shoes pointing out at forty-five degree angles from vertical.

"Seems to be," she said.

McGruder lowered his voice to a whisper. "Where is she?"

Haldeman only betrayed surprise by raising his right eyebrow. "Where's who?"

"That blonde kid," whispered McGruder. "The girl he was with."

"I'm not sure," said Dean, with considerable aplomb. "Does she have a name?"

"How would I know her name?" came the furious whisper. "Hell, he probably didn't know her name. Just a chubby little blonde with a white shirt and tan shorts. One of the crowd that follows him around."

"So, why do you think she's here?" asked Dean.

"I think we all know the answer to that," hissed McGruder. "We've got to keep this quiet, for God's sake. We can't have this getting out. It's bad enough that he had a heart attack. I kept telling him, you know, 'not right after you eat,' for God's sake." He looked at Haldeman, beseechingly. "I tried to tell him, it's just like swimming."

Haldeman glanced at Dean and saw her turn away. That meant he could not, and he made an enormous effort to control his expression and voice. "We appreciate that you tried to warn him," he said. "Should wait an hour, I understand."

He heard a squeak from Dean, and ignored it. "So, this girl was with him the last time you saw him?"

"Oh yes. Blackwell was supposed to speak tonight at the Young Republicans' dinner. I'm the one that had to hustle Mrs. Blackwell out of the way so he could have his fun."

"Well, Mr. McGruder," said Haldeman, "you might take some solace in what I'm going to tell you."

"What?"

"He appears to have been shot."

McGruder's face went blank for a moment as it sank in. "Well, Thank God!" he said, with considerable relief. Then his expression changed. "Shot?"

"It would appear so."

"And that was the cause of death?"

"Well," said Haldeman, "the Medical Examiner hasn't seen him, but it's a good guess."

"But who would have done that?"

Haldeman permitted himself a smile. "That's the question we've just been asking ourselves," he said. ✤

✤ As it turned out, two hours later it was a question they were still asking. The M.E. had arrived and had discovered an exit wound in the back of the corpse. An apparent exit wound. One couldn't be absolutely sure until the autopsy. Through and through, though. No doubt about that. Obviously the bullet had contained enough energy to pass completely through the victim. This made it unlikely it had been a handgun. A quick examination of Blackwell's providentially white shirt had revealed absolutely no discoloration from the powder that would indicate a shot in close proximity to the deceased. Both Zachary Carlton and Shara Hemingly had been interviewed, and aside from several males they'd assumed were some sort of Secret Service, they had nothing to offer. Dean had patiently explained to them that there was no security provided by the state to candidates, with the exception of the incumbent governor who had declined to run who rated one State Trooper. Therefore, all the "security" people were of interest. The young couple was taken to the local police department where they would provide written statements. Homer McGruder was sent to join them.

Haldeman and Dean had instructed the uniformed officers to fan out and look for a chubby blonde female in a white blouse and tan shorts. So far nothing had come of the search. The DCI mobile crime lab unit was enroute from Des Moines. Three more DCI officers were at the scene, along with a Sheriff's investigator and two local police detectives.

They'd stood the body upright and tried to determine the direction of the shot. It was likely from the north, or northwest, but it was uncertain. There were a couple of scuff marks near the body, and it was possible that he'd spun after taking the hit. Haldeman and Dean took a short break with two cups of watered-down lemonade the EMT's had scrounged from a nearby stand.

"You know what bothers me?" asked Dean.

"What?"

"She had to know what was up, didn't she?"

Haldeman nodded. "You mean the groupie?" He took a sip of the awful drink. "Yeah, I think she did. Nobody could have stumbled on the fact that he'd be in that secluded sort of spot. He was led."

"So that means a conspiracy of at least two."

"Well, in Iowa I believe it might take three"

"You know what I mean," said Dean.

"For him to be set up, somebody had to know he was—what—susceptible to that sort of thing. Just before a speech, for heaven's sake."

"Cheerleaders."

"Right." Dean set her cup down on the concrete wall.

"Somebody who had to know him pretty well, somebody who

had to know how he'd react. How he'd be able to be convinced to do that."

She looked around. "And somebody who knew this area well enough to know there was a perfect spot. Secluded, yet with an opening for a long range shot." They both began walking to the blood stained patch of grass where Blackwell had died.

"The clear shot is a problem," said Dean.

"I admit that."

"Well," said Haldeman. "We're talking lots of energy. But, say, 400 yards—high powered rifle with a scope. That'd do it." They stopped together, one on each side of the stain. They both looked out to the North.

"Top floor of that brick building over there," said Dean.

"Or the roof," said Haldeman. "That'd do it." ❖

❖ Ten minutes later they were on the roof of 12 Erlichman Plaza, looking across the tops of the trees, directly into the cordoned off area of the crime scene. Haldeman knelt down, resting his elbow on the black steel rail that encircled the flat roof. "Perfect," he said, in a conversational tone. "I could hit him from here, open sights. Piece of cake. But I don't think we could see over the tree tops from the floor below. Has to be the roof for a reliable shot."

"But only if you knew he'd be there," said Dean. "We can't see the area where the Young Republicans were going to meet. Not from here." They were silent for a few moments. "If I was to do this one," she continued, "if I was to make the effort to do this, I'd want a shooter at more than one location. Wouldn't you?"

"I dunno," said Haldeman.

"That takes resources."

"Somebody with an organization . . . ." She let the sentence trail off. They were both quiet again, thinking thoughts they really didn't want to think. Haldeman spoke first.

"The Attorney General's office is gonna hate this one. Too much like the Kennedy assassination."

"You mean too much like the crazy theories that came after," said Dean. She grimaced. "We're really going to have to have all the little ducks in a row on this one. Just to start."

"Which brings us back to the essential question." He smiled. "Who done it?"

They contacted the Crime Scene Team via portable radio and requested an ID team come to the roof to gather any possible evidence. There likely wouldn't be any. They had to remain on the roof until the arrival of the team, to "preserve" the scene. Haldeman found himself toeing the graveled rooftop, hoping to uncover something, anything that would give them a link to the shooter.

"A pro would pick up his rounds," said Dean. "You're just wasting your time."

"Helps me think," he replied, not looking up.

"Right." He could hear the smile in her voice. "At least something does."

"Somebody in the building probably heard something, don't you think?"

"Yeah. We better get on that as soon as we can."

Haldeman worked his way slowly back to the edge where the shooter must have been.

"Done thinking," Dean asked, "or do you want to start a second lap?"

"Why did somebody want him dead?"

She shrugged. "Want a list?"

"Yeah."

"Well, he was a career politician. That's one. He was an attorney. That's two. He was in the lead, so that's three." She grinned. "Wasn't he the one who told the hog lot protesters that the smell they were complaining about was 'the smell of gold'?"

"He was."

"Well, hell, I would just about have done it for that one."

He chuckled. She wouldn't have, of course. But it was a point well taken. "Somebody he pissed off, then, you think?"

"Big time."

"Had to be somebody with resources."

"Let's not rule out a purely political motive," said Dean. "I mean, we always think of the overthrow of a government for political motive, but how about leadership of a party?"

"Good old fashioned power play?"

"Well, yeah." She looked defensive, prompted by his tone. "What?"

"Mick, this is Iowa. Get real."

She hesitated a moment. "I suppose so. Yeah, you're right. We better find the blonde and find her fast. She's the key." She gazed off toward the park. "What a sleaze. His wife here and everything. Gets himself killed by sneaking off into the bushes with some bimbo."

"You don't suppose?" he offered.

"The wife?" she asked. "Well, it's about as traditional a motive as you'll ever get."

He spread his hands. "Best motive in the world."

"Too cold-blooded," said Dean. "This is a hit. Not a murder. A bona fide hit." ✚

✚ They spent the next nine hours interviewing everybody they could find who had been in the building at 12 Erlichman Plaza. Nobody had heard a thing. And, in the meantime, Zachary and Shara were wishing they'd never sought a moment's seclusion in People's Park.

DONALD HARSTAD *now writes fulltime, but from 1970 to 1996 he served in the Clayton County Sheriff's Department in roles ranging from police dispatcher to chief investigator.*

Don draws regularly on this rich experience for characters and plots for his fiction. His novels include Eleven Days *(1998),* Known Dead *(1999), and* Big Thaw *(2000). His yet unnamed fourth and fifth novels have already been purchased by Doubleday/Bantam in the United States and by Fourth Estate in the United Kingdom.*

Although he was born in Los Angeles, Don met his wife, Mary, in Elkader, Iowa, and they dated throughout high school. They married in 1965 and moved to Los Angeles where Don worked for Four Star Television and CBS Theatrical Films. The Harstads returned to Iowa in 1970 to raise their daughter, Erica. They reside in Elkader where Mary teaches school and Don writes and keeps in touch with local law enforcement.

3.

Will the Real Bob Blackwell Please Stand Up?

By Ken Sullivan

Not until a few minutes after the first couple of squad cars screeched to a halt a dozen yards or so from the cooling remains of Bob Blackwell did Drew Wright stir from behind the lilac bushes, lush with huge, fragrant purple blossoms. A single officer was posted near the body, while three others secured the scene, stringing a yellow "crime scene" tape from tree to tree. They would be making a preliminary investigation, but the detailed probe of the scene, the surroundings, and the body would be handled by the DCI.

Wright hadn't been more than 50 feet from them when college lovebirds Shara and Zachary stumbled onto the body, but, unlike others who'd come to People's Park for a day of serenity and recreation, Wright wasn't drawn like a magnet by the coed's horrified shrieks. Out of habit, he'd chosen to step back and try to create an image in his mind of details others might miss.

The upended trash container, for example. The broken limb on one of the white pine trees near Blackwell's corpse. The reaction of the crowd to the young woman's shrieks. The surge of people in the direction of the noise. Except for a girl, who seemed confused. Wright hadn't seen her initially, but spotted her in the background, perhaps 30 or 40 feet from the body, the instant he turned his head in the direction of Shara Hemingly's scream. While others moved toward the sound of the anguished cries, the young woman paused momentarily, then moved in the opposite direction, first tentatively, then in all-out flight.

Wright might have dismissed her reaction as that of one who is disturbed by violence. Except for a fleeting moment when it occurred to him that she was familiar. "Where?" he wondered, immediately pigeon-holing the incident and the image for later.

Within minutes local police officers had arrived, two squad cars sliding to a gravel-spewing halt a dozen yards or so from the earthly remains of Bob Blackwell. With their arrival, Wright inched closer, not because of the morbid fascination that attracted other horrified spectators, but to continue his examination of the scene and the people.

He avoided eye contact, instead scanning each face briefly. He absorbed disjointed snippets of conversation, evaluated them for potentially useful information, then discarded extraneous matter. Nodding to a couple of officers he'd met during his early years as a police reporter at the *Cedar Falls Record*, he hoped they'd accept his presence as official business and not shuffle him behind the yellow tape as they were other onlookers. What they didn't know, Wright reasoned, wouldn't hurt them. Yet, he adroitly avoided getting in any officer's way. The fewer questions they asked, the better for him.

Others, not "privileged" to rate such a first-hand glimpse of violence and gore as he had during more than a decade as a newspaper reporter, were imprinting the scene in their memories. What they saw was ammunition they'd use for weeks to become the center of attention in their various circles of acquaintance, Wright was sure. As for his account of Bob Blackwell's demise, that would have to wait.

His story would be told, he was confident, but on his terms.

And what a story it promised to be because he knew a lot more about the man than did those admiring Iowans who seemed to want Blackwell for their next governor.

Wright had begun the campaign season as a reporter with *The Cedar Rapids Bulletin*, one of the state's foremost newspapers. As the first few men and woman entered the Republican primary, he viewed the race with ambivalence, another campaign with maybe one or two marginally qualified candidates and a bevy of nut cases who couldn't win a blood test if they knew the answers. All most wanted was the 15 minutes of fame and glory they figured was their due.

And then Blackwell announced.

The bar was raised immediately, thought Wright who, at 34, was with his third newspaper in 12 years, moving up the professional ladder in Iowa. Each assignment was more challenging than the last, but Wright tried to learn the craft at each rung on the ladder. With Blackwell's declaration as a candidate for the Republican nomination for governor, Wright knew for certain years of grunt work were about to be rewarded.

Becoming governor would have been the ultimate achievement for Robert Blackwell, Wright decided, because he gave the current Iowa Secretary of the Treasury credit for recognizing there were limits on the gullibility of the public. A Cedar Rapids contractor with a law degree who had steadily risen in Republican politics, Blackwell had managed for years to portray himself to voters as a caring, compassionate humanitarian who put his constituents' needs ahead of personal ambition.

How he'd managed to delude so many people for so long was a constant source of amazement to Wright. The reporter knew better, but compiling evidence was taking longer than he'd anticipated.

Wright saw in Blackwell's candidacy an opportunity to serve justice. Though Iowa was the center of the political universe during its presidential precinct caucuses every four years, the state faded into the woodwork during intervening years. Political scandal in the off-year election of 2002 had the potential to restore Iowa to national political attention. Negative publicity, to be sure, but Wright figured the state had to be prepared to take some of the bad along with the good.

"And it couldn't happen to a better guy," Wright reasoned as he began to build the case he believed would derail Blackwell's political ambitions.

It was in November that Blackwell offered himself as a candidate for the GOP nomination in the June 2002 primary. He could have been the poster child for sincerity and humility, Wright recalled.

"I feel your pain," Blackwell had said, assuming Iowans weren't clever enough to know he'd borrowed that particular banality from Bill Clinton. He'd hit every hot button on the political scoreboard: education, health care, land use, environmental protection, better farm prices, lower taxes, and more tourist attractions. Positioning himself as one of those "compassionate conservatives," he hemmed, hawed, and mumbled whenever abortion, firearms, and capital punishment were raised.

"Hell," Wright had grumbled to fellow reporters covering Blackwell's announcement rally, "if this guy gets elected with that BS, he deserves an Oscar for pulling the wool over the public's eyes. The SOB belongs in jail. Or hell!"

The next three months were as close to routine as statewide campaigns can be. The first speech of the week set the tone for each candidate's activities until the following week. Variations on the same message would be delivered in various venues for the next six days. A higher education speech to students at Iowa State University on a Monday morning could be manipulated into a declaration of undying support for educational excellence to the Iowa State Education Association's spring meeting in Des Moines the following Saturday.

That gave Wright the freedom he needed to probe his suspicions about Blackwell and to reconfirm that which he knew to be true.

It was in March that he approached his editors at *The Bulletin* with a thick file folder of facts, circumstantial evidence, and suspicions. He had plenty to work with.

Wright, for example, was one of very few who knew about the vacation getaway Blackwell owned in the Canadian wilderness. "Just a shack where I can get away from the phones—and you darn reporters," Blackwell said, his lips arced into a grin, but his eyes hard and cold. The "shack" shown in the photograph that had come into Wright's possession was a three-story dwelling, native stone, huge fireplace, lakefront, and complete with its own generator. Price? Just so happens a grateful commercial developer for whom Blackwell had done favors offered the "shack" at a deep discount, approximately a dime on the dollar. The legality of the transaction would need a court's judgment, but Wright was confident those adoring voters who believed the state's Treasurer could do no wrong might view that sweetheart deal as something of an epiphany.

Wright had no illusions about the barrage of rebuttal his allegations would encounter, however. He'd been in the business long enough to know even the threat of a libel suit raised alarms in every newsroom. That's why he took more chances than he should have. It wasn't a problem to find disgruntled former employees who painted Blackwell as a phony, a hypocrite. However, cross-examination might make mincemeat of them.

Stronger evidence came from close aides who'd become disenchanted with Blackwell over the years; they portrayed him as a tyrant, a bigot, a sexist. And Wright had gotten verification from a few still on Blackwell's staff, those whose own loyalty was based on the size of their paycheck.

Any doubts Wright may have had about those leaks vanished

during his interview with Blackwell's top aide, Nels Bellaci. They met in February at state campaign headquarters in Des Moines, ostensibly so Wright could get background information for a profile he planned to write for the gubernatorial primary.

Wright kept his micro-cassette recorder in his pocket. Running. And, rather than rehash clichés about the primary or revisit biographical information about Blackwell he knew by heart, he hit the ground running. Bellaci sparred at first. Deflected the questions. Challenged the motives of the accusers. But only occasionally did he specifically speak to an assertion. There were many:

"I'm told he's racist," said Wright. Nothing.

"He got rich by taking bribes," Wright claimed. Silence.

"He's a fake, a phony and a hypocrite," Wright shouted.

At last, Bellaci responded.

"Don't get in over your head, my friend," he said, his voice threatening and his eyes piercing. "You manage to get one word of this in print and you'll regret the day you learned to spell. No two-bit word butcher is going to threaten us. We'll see you in hell first."

For three days, Wright weighed Bellaci's threat. On the fourth day, confident that Blackwell's people wouldn't dare touch him once the truth was out, he met with Managing Editor Ernie Crossman to make his case for a multi-part exposé on the real Bob Blackwell. He didn't tell Crossman about the threat, but instead itemized the irregularities, contradictions, and inconsistencies he considered damning evidence against Blackwell.

For starters, he was prepared to claim—and prove—that the current Secretary of the Treasury and odds-on favorite to become the next governor of Iowa was a racist, contrary to his public declarations. "I have evidence that his former Cedar Rapids construction firm didn't employ a single minority in a position of responsibility. He hired only a few minorities—as laborers. I won't even say the word he calls them. And that's not hearsay. I was in his campaign office a few years ago when he was running for the county board, and heard him talking to one of his foremen who had come in to report that one of the African-American laborers had ruined a concrete footing. I was embarrassed just to be hearing what he said.

"And he's an equal opportunity bigot. I have statements that show he hates Asians, Hispanics . . . anybody who doesn't look like him. I'm still working on it, but I've been told he's the one who planted the rumor two years ago about his opponent, Joseph Ahn, being a child molester. I don't think it's just a coincidence that Ahn's an Asian-American.

"You got one of those anonymous information packets that claims Blackwell's a Nazi, or a Nazi-sympathizer. The one item that intrigues me is the one that claims he's blackballed Catholics and Jews from membership in his country club. If all that stuff is true, hell, if half of it's true, voters should be told.

"And that's not all. His company makes a big deal out of contributing a couple of grand a year to AIDS research. But do you know what he really believes? I taped one of his advisers who bragged that Blackwell considers AIDS a just reward for 'homos and druggies.' They deserve what they get, he thinks. Why should taxpayers have to take care of them? Or their kids? It's on tape, boss. That's from his own people.

"When he talked to the Citizens Against Firearms in Iowa City last week, he swore to support anything the Legislature sent him to control ownership of handguns, but if you look at this record from the Campaign Finance office, you'll see he's taken a $10,000 contribution from the National Rifle Association.

"I have page after page of this stuff. At best the guy's a hypocrite and a liar. I think we can prove he's a thief, too. With what I have here—and it will be better if you can give me another couple of weeks to check out these other tips—we can take this guy out.

It'd be a public service."

Crossman had been noncommittal throughout the presentation. He'd been in the business a long time and had worked with a lot of eager-beaver young reporters who were convinced they had a Pulitzer Prize by the tail. He'd been one of them, in fact. Thirty years ago, or so. Wright hadn't expected an instant directive. He certainly hadn't expected the answer he got the following day.

"Drop it," said Crossman.

"I can't."

"It's either that, or . . . "

"Or what?"

"Do I really need to tell you?"

In all his years as a reporter, Wright had wondered how he'd stand in a battle between principles and pragmatism. What he envisioned, of course, was a showdown between him and authorities who demanded his testimony or notes or eyewitness account of an incident to help make their case against a private citizen. He'd never been sure how he'd respond when given the option of compliance or jail for contempt of court.

When Crossman delivered the ultimatum, he knew. He refused to quit. He refused to back away from his Blackwell probe.

He was fired.

That happened weeks ago, two months, actually, and it had taken about half that time for Wright to come to grips with reality. He didn't blame Crossman. The chain of command in any newspaper calls for the reporter to talk to the editor and the editor to talk with his or her editor and on up the ladder to the publisher, who, despite a lack of experience in the newsroom, has the final voice in what appears in the paper. Usually that isn't a problem, because publishers tend to focus their attention on revenue-producing elements of their operations, rather than the newsrooms; unless, of course, editors got too squirrelly in sending reporters out to far-flung locations for exotic assignments.

When a powerful elected official's reputation was on the line, however, and especially an official with whom the publisher was known to socialize, only an editor with a death wish would fail to adhere to protocol and consult the guy who signs his paycheck. Blackwell's warts weren't going to find their way into *The Bulletin*.

Wright's gloom was short-lived. When word of his unemployment got out, newspapers from New York, Washington and Chicago signed him on as a stringer for the gubernatorial primaries that spring. Not only did it put a few hundred bucks a month into a seriously depleted checking account, but this stringer arrangement could help get his foot into the door for a job in the big leagues. Especially if he could sell one of the papers, or all three, what he knew to be the real story about the Republican front-runner.

But now, as he watched officers in People's Park go through their painstaking routine, Wright wondered what part of the "real story" of Blackwell he had missed. And, dammit, who was that girl?

KEN SULLIVAN *retired in February after 36 1/2 years with the* Cedar Rapids Gazette *and more than 40 years as a journalist, including stints with the* Oelwein Daily Register *and KCHA-Radio in Charles City. For the last 22 years he has been a political writer and, later, senior editor at* The Gazette. *He's covered every presidential, gubernatorial, senate, and congressional campaign since 1980.*

4.

Memorial Day
at Iowa's Great Lakes

By Ann Struthers

The warm and enticing smells of barbecue rose over Pikes
Point State Park and floated out over Lake Okoboji. It was late in
the afternoon, a beautiful Memorial Day Sunday. The Dickinson
County Republicans had hung up red, white, and blue banners
between the trees. The ladies were busy taping white paper over
the picnic tables and weighting down the paper plates and nap-
kins with pickle jars and catsup bottles.

A strong breeze was blowing from the east as Lt. Scott Dallas,
commander of the Iowa State Patrol, wandered about the
grounds. He wasn't on duty and didn't need to be there. He and
his wife, Charlie, were on vacation, staying across the lake at
Crandall's Beach.

"You should relax, have fun, get on your bike and come with
me." She was riding in the Memorial Day twenty-mile ride
around Spirit Lake sponsored by the mythical University of
Okoboji. But with one candidate for the governor's race already
murdered and another one just last weekend nicked by flying
glass when a stray bullet hit her windshield, Lt. Dallas couldn't
stay away.

Ever since the Great RAGBRAI murders two summers before,

a case which he had worked on extensively, he had been even more dedicated to his work than before. Of course, he knew most crimes weren't solved in the approximately 20 minutes TV allots its characters. He knew many investigations drag on for years. What was required was painstaking dredging, a careful assembling of small details, taking down information from everyone who might or might not have a clue.

Mostly they didn't have a clue. He sighed, remembering no matter how much good police work is done, just as often as not it's a lucky break that eventually leads to the culprit and to his or her conviction. He also knew that if Bob Blackwell had been murdered for political reasons, it was more than likely the perpetrator would be at this rally.

So far the police in Cedar Falls had been stymied in their investigation. They had eventually brought in a chubby girl, who almost fit the description Homer McGruder, Blackwell's campaign manager, had given them. It turned out she worked at the 7-11 and had been on duty all day and had two witnesses to prove it. Lt. Dallas smiled, thinking about the Cedar Falls police and the DCI bending a suspicious eye on all the fat girls in the town.

Lt. Dallas wandered down to the Point itself and sat on some rocks dumped there by the glacier millions of years ago, looking out at the blue water. Lake Okoboji was one of only three blue-water lakes in the world, blue because of an algae that lived in its depths. It was a deep lake, more than 200 feet in places. In fact, the safe swimming water at the right was carefully delineated with red plastic ropes floating on buoys. Just beyond the ropes was a steep drop off into more than 100 feet of water. The water was cold, too.

Charlie and he had been swimming every day since they came, but he had to plunge in quickly and swim as hard as he could to warm up. Even then he came out shivering. Well, refreshed, too. Right now there were at least one hundred kids playing in the sand and splashing in the water. Mothers were herding and chucking at them. Teenage girls, carefully oiled, were spread out on their beach towels. Teenage boys ran among the groups, hoping the girls would notice them. They were giving the concession stand in the big old stone and timber shelter house a good income today. Here and there older Iowans sat under umbrellas and read *The Des Moines Register*, struggling with the wind which snatched at the papers.

"Lt. Dallas," a voice said behind him. Dallas knew he had heard the voice before, but he didn't place it. He turned slowly and there was Homer McGruder, holding out his hand. Dallas shook hands and said "I thought your man dropped out of the race."

McGruder ignored the joke. "Well, you know how it is," he said. "Frankly, the party was stunned. Yes, sir, stunned. Blackwell was their man, and well, the others . . . ." His voice trailed off.

"I should think Mrs. Louella Strong would really appeal to the farm vote," Dallas said.

"Well, you know, she's really too radical. She's been too outspoken against hog lots."

Lt. Dallas nodded. He didn't want to say what he thought about enormous hog lots.

"Lots of farmers want to make a few bucks setting up hog operations with the big farm corporations. It's a question of whether I can use my land the way I want to or not. Is this a free country or isn't it?"

"I don't suppose the party likes Jim Taverus, either," Lt. Dallas said. Taverus had continued to spew his version of white supremacy and had invited David Duke, the Louisiana politician who was also an officer in the Ku Klux Klan, to a rally he held down in Oskaloosa. As it turned out, David Duke hadn't showed and almost nobody else did either.

"Taverus is dangerous," McGruder said. "I wouldn't touch him with a ten-foot pole."

"McGruder, McGruder." Two people were calling him. Zachary Carlton and Shara Hemingly were loping across the lawn toward them.

"Who are they?" Dallas asked.

McGruder shaded his eyes. "Oh, it's the two college kids from Cedar Falls who found Blackwell. Met them at that awful time. Nice kids."

"Are they suspects?" Dallas asked.

"Couldn't be," McGruder said. "The boy's interested in politics. The girl's a kind of idealistic radical. Not practical."

The two young people shook hands with McGruder and he introduced them to Dallas, not mentioning his name or profession. Dallas was grateful for that. McGruder may have crossed them off the suspects list, but Lt. Dallas never crossed off anyone until the real perpetrator was safely convicted and behind bars.

"I heard you were managing the campaign of Ed Van Der Boomsma," Zach said.

The state Republican party had been thrown into a tailspin after Blackwell's murder. While it is a free country, and anyone can run for office, McGruder and the Republican hierarchy had decided they quickly had to find a presentable conservative candidate—the others, especially Taverus, didn't have enough general appeal. The party regulars were afraid there were still a lot of people out there who wouldn't vote for a woman for governor and besides, Louella Strong's vehement campaigning against hog lots had alienated a lot of the big corporate contributors. Carmelita Lopez's emphasis on minorities and higher wages for the Hispanic packing house workers would alienate the conservatives in the state who were wary of "foreigners" and generally thought the packing house workers already made good wages. That had left the young priest. He was anti-abortion which appealed to many in the party. He was in favor of posting the Ten Commandments in public buildings including schools, in favor of prayer in the schools, and for beautification of the state, and his campaign slogan was "Violets not Violence." He spoke in beautiful abstract phrases about Iowa's strong common culture, Iowa's reverence for life, Iowa's love of the land.

At a secret meeting of the party's steering committee, McGruder had told the head honchos, "Idealism is all well and good in its place, but what this party needs is someone who will strongly support the NRA, who is pledged to support business in Iowa, including the large corporate farms, especially the factory hog farms, and someone who will fight the unions. This priest is probably pretty good as a philosopher, but we need a really practical man."

The chairman had agreed with McGruder. "You can't trust a clergyman," he said. "They always say they're practical, but they always end up wanting to help the poor. This state can't afford any more aid to the poor." The party leaders had agreed and at McGruder's suggestion had given their secret blessing to the new candidacy of Edward Van Der Boomsma.

Although he was entering the primary very late, the party rounded up a great deal of money to pour into his campaign. Soon everyone in the state who had a TV set knew that Edward Van Der Boomsma was a farmer from Pella, that he was also a businessman, owning several grain elevators in small Iowa towns, and that he was four-square for everything that was four-square. A tall silver-haired man with a booming voice, he looked like a governor and, with McGruder running his campaign, it was beginning to look as if, despite the nasty mess of a murder in April, that the Grand Old Party had come up with another winner.

"So you came to hear the speeches?" McGruder inquired of the two college kids.

"I came to see Shara," Zach Carlton said.

"My folks have a cottage at Arnold's Park," Shara said, "but Zach can't stay away from politics—so we're here."

"I think you'll hear a great speech today," McGruder said in his best official candidate's voice.

Lt. Dallas surveyed the two young people. They looked inno-cent enough. But he knew that looks are deceiving. He had seen more than one baby-faced murderer.

They all wandered back to the small podium draped in bunting. Taverus began to speak. "Your ancestors built this state. They built it from nothing. Bare prairie. Hard work. Back breaking work. But they weren't afraid of work, and they worked hard, night and day, and they built well for us to enjoy. But do we want all this taken away from us by foreigners? I tell you the United States government, those namby-pamby bureaucrats in Wash-ington, will let anyone into this country. They let in the guys who blew up the World Trade Center in New York. Anyone with an ounce of sense would know that these guys were dangerous. How many more dangerous foreigners have they let in? Do we know who killed Bob Blackwell? My friends, I can tell you that disrupt-ing the elections in the United States is high on the agenda of these foreign agents. Why there may be assassins roaming around even here today. We have to stand up for our rights against all these people who are trying to take over the United States. White men built this country. White men built Iowa. I say, vote for Taverus and stand up for the people you can trust!"

There was little applause. The sun was hot and Taverus loos-ened his tie and stepped down from the platform and walked out into the audience and began shaking hands with the listeners who were sitting on folding chairs they had brought along or on the picnic benches.

Mrs. Strong spoke next. She was a heavy-set farm wife, her steel gray hair cut short, her steel gray eyes sharp and penetrat-ing behind her wire-rimmed glasses. She looked as if she'd be right at home in an apron serving at a church supper—or equally at home riding a tractor in one of her fields. Indeed, she had done both. She was obviously annoyed at Taverus. "I want to say a few things about the people who built this state. Many people built Iowa. My great-grandmother drove a team of horses, pulling a plow when my folks first came to Buena Vista County in 1880. Everyone in that family and all the succeeding families worked, men, women, children. It took all of them to build this country. And I remember the blacksmith in Rose Center—a blacksmith who was a black man, and the best blacksmith around. He helped build this country, too, and so did his family. One of his sons went on to become a doctor at University Hospitals. I remember my friend Danny Big Bear from Tama, the drummer in the famous rock band, Broken Arrows. He built music into this country. It takes all kinds of people to build a society. I won't have any of them left out. It took a lot more than white men."

A number of women in the crowd clapped and cheered.

"But what I really want to talk about is the family farm, and the small family businesses in our small towns, both farms and towns fading away."

Lt. Dallas noted that Shara and Zach had wandered off to the fringes of the crowd.

The speeches went on. Carmelilta Lopez spoke about balancing the state budget. Lt. Dallas thought what she said sounded very sensible, but the day was sunny and bright, the happy shouts of the children on the beach drifted back to the political meeting, and the crowd stirred somewhat restlessly. It was difficult to get people interested in a balanced budget, no matter how much good fiscal management was needed. Actually Dallas had expected her to talk about the packing house workers, but Lopez obviously had a number of issues on her mind, and she outlined them carefully and completely. It was too logical for the crowd, Dallas thought, glancing around.

The young priest was sitting in the front row with a sheaf of papers in his hand. He was leaning forward eagerly, as if he were anxious to speak. Lt. Dallas circled the crowd slowly. There were a large number of people in attendance. Someone had told him earlier that the Iowa Bar Association was meeting at the New Inn this weekend, and he saw a number of faces in the crowd that could only belong to lawyers. He concluded there were probably some tourists there also, people who had come to picnic and stayed to hear what was going on at the rally.

Of course, the local Republicans were out in force. To the right of the podium there was a picnic table covered with electric roasters bubbling away with barbecue. They were connected to the electricity in the shelter house with long, heavy-duty orange cords. Dallas noticed there were two people sitting near the podium, but not facing the speakers, rather watching the crowd. He recognized Haldeman and Dean from the DCI. Good, he thought. Watch everybody.

Lt. Dallas caught only parts of the priest's speech, ". . . eradicate hatred from our hearts, build a better society with brotherhood . . . strong education for strong moral lives. . . ."

Then Van Der Boomsma took the microphone. "What this state needs is strong, reliable, honest-to-God leadership. None of this compromising. What's good for Iowa is good for business, and I say vice versa. We don't need bureaucrats; we don't need sob sisters; we don't need bean counters. We need a leader who can lead. Someone who is one of you. I am Iowa born and bred. And except for a trip to Colorado, I'm happy to say that I've never been out of the state."

Lt. Dallas smiled at Van Der Boomsma's joke, and then wondered if it was really a joke after all.

"This is God's country. And I'm happy to live and die here. We don't need Washington telling us what to do. We don't need outsiders telling us what to do. We are going to protect our guns and our right to go hunting." McGruder led the cheers. "We are going to protect our rights to raise whatever we want to raise on our own land." McGruder led the cheers again. "We are going to protect the Farm Bureau." McGruder cheered again, but few joined him this time. Dallas guessed they were getting hungry. In fact, Dallas had to admit to himself that he was getting hungry too.

It was past six o'clock, the time when all good Iowans ate their supper. In fact, when Lt. Dallas checked his watch, it was almost seven. The shadows were getting long. The sun was sinking lower across the bright waves. *The Queen*, a replica of one of the early steamboats that had plied the lakes at the end of the nineteenth century, blew its whistle as it turned to sail across the lake and down the other side.

Numerous speedboats, noisy as mosquitoes, and just about as popular with Lt. Dallas, crisscrossed the waters. Here and there a sailboat spread its white wings.

The serving began. The Hy-Vee workers in their clean white aprons began ladling the barbecue onto buns and adding pickles, baked beans, and potato chips. There were canisters of soft drinks and urns of coffee. The candidates were circulating in the crowd, shaking hands, kissing babies, trying to avoid being stopped by voters with specific problems they wanted solved, or specific projects they wanted either started or banned. Smile, smile, smile. They all smiled. Van Der Boomsma was clapping men on the back. The young priest, who was remarkably good-looking, Lt. Dallas noted, was surrounded by a circle of young women. He was being pleasant, but Lt. Dallas could see he obviously wanted to get away.

Lt. Dallas broke through the girlish ring and placed his loaded styrofoam plate in the young priest's hand. "Come with me, Father," he said, and he led the way to a picnic table on the fringes of the crowd where only two other men were seated. To his surprise, he saw the two were Jim Wade, the mystery writer, and Inspector Reginald Brontey-Blemming from Scotland Yard. Wade had been on the notorious RAGBRAI ride two years before and had courted one of the suspects, not knowing at the time she was involved.

Lt. Dallas introduced them to Father Metterschmidt and Wade explained that he and Inspector Brontey-Blemming had become good friends and that he had invited him to a typical Iowa Memorial Day at the Lakes, a time when they could watch the University of Okoboji's Annual Run, which they had done yesterday, and that evening they were going to go to the high school ball diamond and watch the University's team defeat the baseball teams from Harvard, Yale, and Princeton. The Inspector laughed gleefully. "Jolly good fun," he said. "Greatest imaginary University I've ever seen."

The four of them sat there enjoying the evening air, discussing captains, kings, and sealing wax, and the picnic. The crowd thinned out. Lt. Dallas noticed Carmelita Lopez wander down toward the lake.

The shadows became even longer. Finally Father Metterschmidt excused himself. "I think the politic thing to do is to sample some of that chocolate cake," he said, heading back toward the food tables. He disappeared in the gathering darkness and the crowd.

Lt. Dallas began to worry about Charlie back at Crandall Beach. He hadn't intended to stay this long, but it was good to visit with Wade again who told him he still hadn't found any woman who wanted to share the rest of his life. "I guess they think I'm getting so old I'm looking for a nurse rather than a girl friend," he laughed. Wade was only 45, but Lt. Dallas thought he did look older this year. Maybe all the excitement of the RAGBRAI murders had aged him.

Lt. Dallas ruefully told himself that he, too, had aged. It was pleasant to hear the Inspector's British accent, floating lightly on the Iowa air. They discussed the recent political murder, and the inspector advanced several theories. Wade said it would make a hell of a good book, and he proceeded to outline a plot for it. Finally Father Metterschmidt returned.

Just then they heard some screams from the beach. It was kids yelling, but this wasn't the happy kind of yells they had heard all afternoon. This was scared-the-bejesus-out-of them screams. Lt. Dallas saw detectives Dean and Haldeman race past them toward the noises.

The three of them rose and ran toward it too.

When they got to the water's edge they found Dean and Haldeman dragging a body out of the water. It was Carmelita Lopez!

"Is she dead?" someone asked. Nobody answered, but Haldeman and Dean began giving her artificial resuscitation. Lt. Dallas opened his cell phone and called the Dickinson County sheriff and then his own headquarters. Finally he remembered to call Charlie.

A small crowd had gathered around them, and Lt. Dallas heard Zach Carlton say to Shara, "I wonder what's going on in the Democrats' race."

ANN STRUTHERS *is the Writer-in-Residence in the English Department of Coe College in Cedar Rapids. She recently returned from a stint as a Fulbright Fellow in the Middle East, but she could find no way to work Aleppo, Syria, into this novel. Her poems have appeared in various journals, and she has published two collections of poetry,* Stoneboat *and* The Alcott Family Arrives. *She has also published short stories, has written numerous reviews for* The Des Moines Register *and other publications, and she writes both popular and academic articles. She grew up on a farm in Dickinson County and has a summer cottage on Spirit Lake.*

5.
Down and Dirty with the Democrats

By Shirley Kennett

Bill Haldeman knelt in the sand behind Carmelita Lopez's limp body and cradled her head gently. Her eyes were closed and she looked like she was sleeping. But her chest wasn't rising in a normal breathing rhythm, and his questing hands confirmed she had no pulse. The flowery summer dress she'd worn was plastered to her body, just like his own clothes from swimming out into the water to retrieve her. Her shoes were missing, apparently lost in the water. Her bare feet seemed too personal, and he pulled his eyes away.

Haldeman and his partner, Special Agent Michelle Dean, were totally focused on the woman, ignoring the gathering crowd. They held her life in their hands. Long before the paramedics arrived, Carmelita would be dead if they couldn't get her breathing and circulation going. Every second they delayed, brain cells could be dying from lack of oxygen-rich blood.

The DCI agents were well trained in resuscitation, but it was the first time they'd had to put their skills to use. They might kid around with each other a lot in other aspects of their work, but not in this. Not an unnecessary word was spoken.

"Turn," Dean said.

Haldeman lifted Carmelita's chin and supported her head as
Dean rolled the woman onto her side. Then he opened her mouth.
Water gushed out and soaked rapidly into the sand. He slipped
his fingers into her mouth, pushing down her tongue, making
sure her airway was clear. The coughing and sputtering he was
hoping to hear didn't happen. His hand came away wet from the
back of her head and in the near-darkness he could just make
out that it wasn't from water. There was a bloody wound in the
back of her head. His fingers probed lightly. She'd been hit with
something, maybe a rock picked up from the lakeshore, or she'd
slipped and struck her head. Slipped in ten feet of water? That's
where she'd been floating, face down. And what would she be doing going swimming fully dressed when it was nearly dark? She'd
been outside the safe swimming zone cordoned off with rope and
buoys, too. If it was an accidental fall on the shore, how could
she have gotten out into the deeper water? She would have been
found lying where she fell. No, of course it had to be deliberate.
Someone had struck her and then pushed her out into the water,
letting nature finish the job he or she had started.

They rolled Carmelita onto her back again and Dean straddled
the woman's chest, her knees digging into the sand. Sand! There
weren't any large rocks around. Whoever did it must have carried a rock for some distance, maybe all the way from the glacial
deposits out at the Point, or brought another weapon of some
kind. A rock, though, made for easy disposal in the deep waters
of the lake.

Dean thumped the sprawled form hard in the middle of the
chest, then lowered her ear to listen for breath and heart sounds.

"Nothing. Give her the first two breaths," Dean said. Her
words were objective, right off the resuscitation chart, but her
voice was tight with emotion. Haldeman had seen her in tough
situations before, had seen her discover corpses, press her hand
on bleeding wounds, uncover a body in a home destroyed by ar-

son. But this was getting to her, probably because they'd both listened to Carmelita's speech such a short time ago. Dean had followed her words closely, nodding at the logical points the candidate had made, empathizing with a woman struggling to make a difference in a male-dominated field.

Haldeman pinched Carmelita's nose closed with his fingers, covered her mouth with his—her skin was so cold—and blew, twice. Out of the corner of his eyes he watched her chest rise. Dean gave the first five compressions, pressing hard enough to bend Carmelita's sternum inward. More breaths, more compressions, on the two of them went, blocking out the activity around them. Haldeman had seen Lt. Dallas nearby before beginning resuscitation, and he was confident Dallas would be doing all the right things.

"Check," Dean said. She lowered her ear again, hoping to hear heart sounds, then shook her head.

Where were the paramedics? It was hard, much harder than most people realized, to keep up manual compressions and breathing. The partners were in good physical shape, but Haldeman could see Dean was tiring. In a minute or two it would be time to switch places. They would keep this up, switching to spell each other on the compressions, until help arrived, or they were too exhausted to continue. Fat chance of that. He'd sooner die than give up on someone who had a chance. They were pushing Carmelita's blood around her body, forcing oxygen into her lungs, keeping her brain alive. Haldeman didn't allow himself to think about how bad that wound on the back of her head was.

Carmelita's body jerked and she began to cough. Water gurgled out of her mouth. She was alive! They'd done it; they'd brought her back. Relief sped through Haldeman's body. Dean rolled off and lay on the sand, exhausted. Carmelita was breathing on her own, and her heart was pumping, but she was barely conscious. Someone brought a picnic blanket and handed it to Haldeman, and he spread it over the woman's chilled body and tucked it under her chin. Her eyes fluttered open. She mumbled something, and Haldeman put his mouth next to her ear.

"Hold on, Miss Lopez. Help is on the way," he said, speaking slowly and clearly. "You'll be all right now."

Her eyes opened weakly and seemed to beckon him in the fading light. She had only a tenuous hold on consciousness. He moved his head so that his ear was almost lying on her lips. Air rasped in and out of her mouth; then she spoke again.

"Happy New Year . . ."

She exhaled, and her breath warmed his cheek. Then she was still. ✤

✤ A hand on Haldeman's shoulder firmly moved him aside. "Paramedics," a voice said. "Step away, sir. We'll take over."

Haldeman rose to his feet and moved off a little way, giving them room to work. He listened as the medics quickly examined Carmelita, placed a mask over her face, and began squeezing air into her. "Pupils dilated and fixed," he heard. "Head trauma. . . . Looks bad, real bad. Yeah, transport, and keep up resuscitation anyway. The doc'll make the formal declaration."

Dean sat up and pounded her fists into the sand. "No, dammit! No! She's got to make it!"

Happy New Year . . . It didn't make sense, Haldeman thought. Was it the random utterance of a person on the verge of death—a person with a fatal brain injury—or was it somehow a clue to Carmelita's killer? Had she even seen her killer? If someone came up from behind her, hit her with a rock, and shoved her into the water, did she even get a glimpse of the person?

He wouldn't be getting any answers from Carmelita. ✤

✤ Melissa Anchor gathered up her daughter Amy in her arms, adjusted the tiny golden cross hanging on a delicate chain around the girl's neck, and kissed her.

"Will I see you before bedtime, Mommy?"

"Sure, sweetie. I couldn't let you go to sleep without a big hug and a kiss goodnight." She put her four-year-old down gently.

"Will you kiss Higgins goodnight too?" Amy held up her tattered stuffed bear.

"Of course I will."

Rick Woodward scowled. "Hurry up, will you? The meeting's going to start soon, and we got to get out of here. I don't understand why I always get stuck with the kid."

The little girl looked surprised. Amy had always thought Rick loved to spend time with her. Now those words "stuck with the kid" hung in the air.

"Why Amy gets to go with you because you love kids so much," Melissa said, trying to smooth things over. "And remember, you promised not to smoke."

"Yeah, yeah, let's get going." Rick's tobacco-stained hands reached for Amy. A little twinge of doubt squeezed Melissa's heart. Maybe she shouldn't be leaving her daughter in the company of this man. Then she saw the cross hanging from Rick's neck, and she knew it would be all right. Whatever else Rick was, he was certainly a believer in their mission. He'd keep Amy safe if only for the cause, but that didn't mean he'd be nice to her. He brushed his long blond hair back and tucked it behind his ear, an echo of Amy's movements. But her daughter's hair glistened with health and a fresh shampooing, and Rick's hair smelled of smoke and could use a good washing, like the rest of him.

Melissa waved to her daughter who was sitting next to Rick with a brave but tentative smile on her face, then watched the car disappear down the street. She turned her attention back to the flower arrangement she was working on for the table in the entry foyer. Red roses, white daisies, and blue carnations. The carnations were dyed, but they looked good enough. She tied some red, white, and blue ribbons on the vase and stood back, hands on her ample hips, to look at her patriotic centerpiece. It looked better than she'd expected it to turn out. Flower arranging wasn't her strength, but she'd had to develop a lot of new skills over the past weeks.

"Mel," a familiar voice said from another room, "they're starting to arrive. Claridge's car just pulled up. I think he's got that damn dog with him. What's that dog's name again? And is Edgar closed up someplace? You know what'll happen if he gets a look at that dog."

The voice belonged to Dr. Samuel Vance, a professor of political science at The University of Iowa. At least he used to be a professor. Nowadays he spent most of his time consulting for a moderate Democratic think-tank in Washington, D.C. Dr. Vance had decided to stop talking about politics and practice some instead. His slick presentations, honed during years of college teaching, combined with actual substance in his middle-of-the-road, conciliatory proposals, had won him broad support. He was the leading contender in the Democratic gubernatorial primaries just three days away on the fourth of June.

"Winston," Melissa said. "The dog's name is Winston. And I've put Edgar in the kitchen." Edgar was a fifteen-year-old Maine Coon cat with definite feelings about boxers. Negative feelings. "I still think this meeting should have been held at the Memorial Union."

The University's Iowa Memorial Union overlooked the Iowa River, had restaurants and meeting rooms, and a staff of people who no doubt could produce better flower arrangements than she could. Dr. Vance didn't respond to her jibe about the Memorial Union. Why bother paying for a private dining room there when an aide could just rustle up some drinks and stick a few flowers around for decoration? The man had a strong practical streak. Other people, less kind, would call him cheap, at least where his political rivals were concerned.

Winston Claridge, just then unceremoniously climbing out of a Lexus, was also running for the Democratic candidacy. He was a businessman from Cedar Rapids, the owner of a chain of computer stores about to be franchised in other states. He was on the brink of big-time financial success and hovering on the boundary between the concerns of big business and those of the little person. Lately it seemed he'd made his choice. He wanted to push the party into closer alignment with big business, but it looked like the constituency wasn't having it. Dr. Vance's latest confidential poll put Claridge in last place, which was pretty bad considering that meant he was less popular than a cross-dressing chef, a gay attorney, and a female veterinarian who specialized in exotic animals.

Melissa had thought some of the Republican candidates were flakes, but that was before she got to know the Democratic ones. Not that Dr. Vance was all that bad. She had to catch herself sometimes and remind herself that she had business arrangements with him and his campaign manager, not personal relationships. Keep it all businesslike. Professional. Detached.

The doorbell rang and she hurried to answer it. As one of Dr. Vance's aides, she'd asked to work tonight. It was an ideal time to get the inside story on what was going on in the Democratic ranks. She'd only been hired by Vance's campaign manager three months ago, but she had a knack for insinuating herself into situations and getting close to people. That was one of the chief reasons she'd been hired.

She'd had no trouble getting close to Bob Blackwell. Even though most men considered her a little too heavyset for their tastes, Blackwell wasn't too picky along those lines. She'd almost blown the whole thing, though. She'd been told to expect a photographer springing out of the bushes, snapping pictures of Blackwell caught with his pants down, literally. When Blackwell had dropped to the ground, blood spreading on his white shirt, she had nearly panicked. Nobody had said anything about murder! Then she had gotten hold of herself and at least had the presence of mind to get off her knees and move away from the body. She winced as she remembered backing into a trash container near the bicycle path and turning it over. The noise of that container hitting the ground seemed so loud to her she was sure the sound must have carried far and wide. But no one reacted. Only when a young woman let out a scream did people take notice. Then Melissa had taken off. As far as she knew, no one had seen her.

That hadn't been the case in a mistake she'd made earlier. While she was observing Bob Blackwell, trying to find out the best way to approach him—turned out she hadn't needed any subtlety there—she'd accidentally gotten her photo taken along with him at a ribbon-cutting ceremony. There she was in the newspaper, her surprised face clearly visible over his shoulder as he bent to cut the ribbon. There hadn't been any real repercussions from it, but she'd taken a lot of flak from Rick, and deservedly so. The mission depended upon everyone doing their best, and that meant thinking on one's feet.

Well, it was good to get out of Cedar Falls and come to Iowa City, and especially good that she didn't have to do this job on her knees. She imagined forgiveness for sins in the line of duty only went so far, and she was probably stretching things already.

Winston the dog romped in and put his paws on her chest. She pushed him away, not hard enough to offend his owner, saying what a big doggie he was. Dr. Vance stepped in and led Winston Claridge the candidate out onto the patio .

Winston the dog followed happily, snuffling the carpet and then the patio bricks. She turned away to answer the bell again as Winston headed for the resplendent Japanese irises. Melissa doubted whether the iris bed, which surrounded the patio and set it off from the rest of the expansive grounds, would ever be the same.

The next arrival was Alan Fairfield. He was conservatively dressed, although she suspected that underneath that blue suit he was probably wearing dainty black silk undies he'd selected from his tolerant wife's lingerie drawer. Even though this was a meeting of rivals he was attending, his chef's background compelled him to bring a lovely tray of canapés, artfully arranged on lace doilies, surrounded by fresh rose petals topped with small flowers Melissa couldn't identify. If things went on this way, she'd have to take a botany course.

"The flowers aren't edible," he said by way of greeting. "You should make sure everyone knows."

Fairfield wasn't nearly as lightweight as first impressions would lead a person to believe. He was a serious contender, second in line to Dr. Vance and capable of closing the gap. He was active in party politics, a good player, and had a solid agenda of health care and education reforms, spending programs to shore up the safety net for the state's poor and aged, restrictions on hog lots to protect the interests of both neighbors and the environment—and a dynamo of a wife who not only tolerated his idiosyncrasies but whose political ambitions almost certainly reached far beyond the Governor's residence.

Melissa sometimes thought Mrs. Fairfield—Candy to her many superficial friends—would do anything to put her husband in office, up to and including dirty dealing, mud slinging, accepting contributions from questionable sources, and, if it came down to it, poisoning squirrels in the park. In some ways she and Candy were alike, except Melissa didn't think she could ever get used to a man borrowing her underwear.

She escorted Fairfield out onto the patio after dropping off the tray he'd brought in the kitchen. The weather was mild for

June and the air carried the scent of flowers and freshly mown grass. Breathing it was practically intoxicating. The brick patio had plenty of privacy. Dr. Vance's home in the University Heights area was spacious, tastefully furnished, full of marvelous architectural details like leaded glass bay windows and a stone tower that housed a three-story staircase. Dr. Vance and his wife had raised their children in this prestigious neighborhood, and when his wife died a few years ago, Dr. Vance kept the home for sentimental reasons. He certainly didn't need all those rooms just for himself.

Melissa hadn't known the late Mrs. Vance, but everything she'd heard about the woman had been good. More than good. Mrs. Vance had been the civilizing influence in her husband's life, and now that she was gone, he felt free to engage in all kinds of activities she would have frowned upon, such as cut-throat politics.

Fairfield joined Claridge and Dr. Vance, neatly sidestepping Winston so that the big dog's paws never came to rest on his suit. Melissa went back inside, hoping they wouldn't get down to business until everyone arrived. Hoping she wouldn't miss anything.

When she got back to the entry foyer, the door was open and Dr. Catherine Shark stood there, with Keith Rolling right next to her. They were the last two aspiring candidates expected for tonight's meeting.

"Yoo hoo," Dr. Shark said. "The door was open, so we just let ourselves in. Is everyone else out back?"

Melissa nodded. The pair took off without her, Dr. Shark dragging Rolling along and ignoring Melissa as though she were a hat tree in the foyer. So far no one had even glanced at her floral arrangement, although the wind of Dr. Shark's passing had stirred the ribbons.

Melissa thought Catherine Shark had an unfortunate but appropriate name. The woman was a veterinarian who spurned the furred and feathered familiar pets in favor of the exotic—and mostly cold-blooded—ones. Seemed to fit her personality, too. She was sharp-edged, abrupt, a transplant from New Jersey who didn't realize the effect she had on Iowans. In spite of that, voters took to her because of her bluntness, straightforward zeal for democracy, and seeming disdain for political machinations. She was experienced, with several successful local elections under her belt. Dr. Shark was definitely ready to move to the state level, and she was going about it with the cold, focused determination of her namesake.

Keith Rolling was about as opposite Catherine Shark in personality as it was possible to get. He was warm, sensitive, and concerned, the kind of guy who'd stop to chat and end up inviting you over for dinner. A Vietnam-era veteran, he leaned hard left in his politics. He didn't flaunt his homosexuality, but he didn't hide it either. He had a long-time domestic partner with whom he had a harmonious relationship most heterosexual married couples would envy. He supported a variety of popular causes. Nevertheless, most political analysts thought Iowa wasn't ready for a gay governor. Dr. Vance had made it clear to Melissa that he agreed. He was surprised Rolling had lasted this long in contention, almost up to the primary. But in a few days, Rolling would be just one of those little bumps on Vance's road to the candidacy, political road-kill. There'd been others, candidates who'd dropped out early. Less for Dr. Vance and his campaign manager to worry about.

When Melissa got back out to the patio, that campaign manager was already there. Arliss Harding must have bypassed the standard procedure of announcing his arrival at the front door and simply taken himself around to the back. Typical. If there was a short cut to be taken, an underhanded method to be employed, or a slimy deed to be done, Harding would gravitate toward it like a rat to a rotten egg.

She wondered what Harding and Vance cooked up together in

their private sessions. She hadn't yet managed to insinuate herself into those. What they said in front of her was bad enough.

The players were in place: Vance, Harding, Shark, Fairfield, Claridge, Rolling. The University Heights Six. Seven, if you counted Winston the dog.

She brought out the tray of canapés and took drink requests, wondering if all political aides did such menial work.

"Don't eat the flowers," she warned. The chef nodded, looking at her closely. When she brought out the drinks, she took a seat nearby, ostensibly to be handy for refills. In reality, she was all ears for the conversation.

It flowed swiftly and freely, moving across a number of topics, never delving deeply into any one in particular. Agendas, grandstanding, homey little diversions—it was all there. Melissa suspected Dr. Vance had invited the other candidates to his home to dissuade one or more of them from continuing. It would play well if a candidate dropped out at this point and threw his or her support to Vance.

There was an event scheduled for tomorrow morning, more of a rally than a serious debate. The party faithful were promising a large turnout and offering a sausage breakfast as an incentive in case hearing the candidates wasn't enough of a draw by itself. The event was to be held in a Coralville Dam picnic area, followed by a press-the-hands tour and photo opportunity at the Devonian Fossil Gorge. Melissa was looking forward to that, and hoped she'd be able to swing bringing Amy along.

The Gorge was the result of a dramatic and prolonged overflow of the Coralville Reservoir Spillway during the 1993 flood. A torrent of water tore away tons of rock and carved an "instant" valley into the limestone bedrock. The Corps of Engineers, checking out the damage, discovered a fascinating sight: a view of the Iowa of 375 million years ago. Vast numbers of fossils were laid bare, providing a glimpse into the life that thrived in the coral-rich seas covering Iowa at that time, which had given the city of Coralville its name.

The flood in 1993 happened before Amy was born. It would be great to get a little bit of Iowa history across to her, even though Melissa knew the girl would be more interested in running her hands over the fossils than listening to a history lesson.

As the meeting progressed, Melissa refreshed drinks, appearing at a candidate's elbow without being summoned. It seemed to justify her presence. She didn't want to be noticed and sent away. At dusk, she carried a fireplace lighter to all the mosquito-repellant candles placed around the patio. They glowed like miniature torches. Solar lighting winked on and gently illuminated the area. It was a perfect early summer evening. She could see a few stars through the branches of the oak trees surrounding the house, and a pleasant breeze sprang up. Iowa in June certainly took a person's mind off all those parking lots covered with snow, ice, or slush—take your pick—endured during the winter.

Melissa learned a few interesting things, all of which she'd pass along to Rick Woodward. Rolling had given hints he was going to drop out of the race tomorrow, after the rally, but he had no intention of declaring loyalty to Dr. Vance. Claridge was plowing on to the bitter end, despite the fact it was common knowledge he'd blown his chances by cozying up to big business in such a blatant way. Fairfield seemed smug and a little arrogant, like he knew something the others didn't. Melissa wondered what the polls would show on the eve of the primary. Fairfield and his gung-ho wife probably thought they were going to displace the front runner at the last minute. A valuable piece of intelligence information, if true. Dr. Shark gave away nothing specific, but Melissa learned that in private the woman wasn't as disdainful of political maneuvering as she proclaimed in public. In fact, she could posture with the best of them.

Melissa's thoughts were wandering. She was thinking about

how Amy was spending her evening and looking forward to some time with her at bedtime. Bath, story, talking softly with the lights out, Amy's damp kiss on her cheek. Then she perked up because she noticed the conversation had gotten around to the trouble besetting the Republican candidates. Big time trouble, spelled M-U-R-D-E-R.

"So what do you think about the killings?" Vance asked. A couple of the candidates shifted uncomfortably in their lawn chairs.

"It's a shame," Rolling said. "I wouldn't wish that on anyone, even if they are Republicans."

"One thing I know is that if I were Van Der Boomsma—heaven forbid—I'd sure be watching my back," Dr. Shark said. "It looks to me like somebody's taking out the top contenders, one at a time. That means he's next."

"Think it's somebody within the ranks over there, or just some wacko?" Harding asked. It was the first time Vance's campaign manager had spoken in an unguarded manner all evening. "Assuming those two are mutually exclusive. Anyway, I wouldn't put it past McGruder. He's a power-hungry S.O.B."

Takes one to know one, Melissa thought.

"Word is McGruder hand-picked Van Der Boomsma," Harding continued. "So it's doubtful he'd be the next victim if McGruder is behind the killers. Or maybe he is the killer, but he's reached a good stopping point. He probably wanted to get somebody more pliant than Bob Blackwell, somebody who'd let him pull the strings."

"Or maybe he just got tired of covering things up when Bob couldn't keep his fly zipped," Rolling said. There was a round of laughter.

"Could be the killings are unrelated," Vance said. "Blackwell had enough in his past to spawn half a dozen murderers. It could just as easily have been something connected to his construction business, or an unhappy client from his attorney days. That

Strong woman who got nicked by flying glass from the windshield could've been a victim of road rage. After all, there wasn't a second attempt. And Lopez might've been taken out by the hog lot owners. She came down on them pretty hot and heavy."

"Yeah, sure," Claridge said. "And if anybody believes that load of bull, I have some stock I'd like to unload." No one even snickered, but Winston the boxer voiced his approval of his master's humor with a loud bark. It paid to have someone around whose loyalty was unquestioned.

"There's another possibility," Rolling said into the thoughtful silence that followed Winston's bark. "And I think it's interesting that nobody's mentioned it."

"What's that, Rolling? The KGB?" Shark said.

"Nope," Rolling said, sipping his iced tea. "One of us did it."

"Huh?" said Claridge.

"Makes sense, kind of," Rolling continued. "Whoever wins the primaries next Tuesday has to face off in the general election, which means all of us sitting around the table here have a stake in who comes out on top over in the Republican camp."

"Meaning we'd want the Republican to win whom we think we'd have the best chance of beating," Claridge said. All eyes fastened on Vance.

"Hey, how come everybody's looking at me?" Vance said.

"You've probably got the most at stake, although you didn't hear it from me," Rolling said. "And maybe because you're just enough of a power freak to do something like that."

Yup, that cinched it. If Rolling dropped out of the race tomorrow, as he'd hinted, he sure wasn't going to throw his support to Vance. There was no love lost between the two of them.

"Or you, Harding," said Fairfield, who'd been keeping his mouth shut, taking it all in. "It would just be another line on your résumé. Probably a few murders on there already, tucked under Professional Achievements."

"Or you, Dr. Shark," Claridge said. "Word's out that you're a cold fish. Get it? Cold fish." Mercifully Winston didn't bark, so there must be some limits to even a dog's loyalty.

"Not me," Shark said. "Personally I'd point the finger at Fairfield's wife, Candy. Now there's a piece of work. I think she'd knock off her own parents if she could shoehorn her dear hubby into office."

After that the conversation died out and never recovered. The esteemed politicians had run out of people to skewer. There was a round of practiced handshakes and then they took their leave. But Melissa had plenty to add to her report to Rick. It had been a most productive evening.

Melissa went home to her daughter. She took the red, white, and blue flower arrangement with her, since no one else seemed to appreciate it. Amy was delighted with it, and in the morning Melissa wove the ribbons into her daughter's shiny blonde hair. It was going to be a lovely day, and she'd decided she was definitely taking Amy with her to the sausage breakfast and then to the Devonian Fossil Gorge event. If Rick complained, she'd tell him next time he would be the one waiting hand and foot on a group of backbiting politicians, and she'd get "stuck with the kid."

She hadn't forgotten he'd said that, and doubted Amy had either.

SHIRLEY KENNETT *has been a mystery fan since she first held a book right-side-up and discovered those squiggles meant something. She's the author of a series of suspense novels featuring PJ Gray, a psychologist and pioneer in the emerging fields of forensic computer simulation. PJ and verteran cop Leo Schultz explore a killer's mind and methods via virtual reality, while coping, more or less, with each other's dynamic personalities and their own family crises. The PJ Gray series includes* Gray Matter, Fire Cracker, Chameleon, *and* Act of Betrayal *(the fourth book written as Morgan Avery). A former resident of Iowa City, Shirley now lives in Missouri with her husand and two sons. They are outnumbered by their cats, two to one.*

6.

Primary Day

By David Yepsen

Brian Cunningham was shining the glasses behind the bar at 801 Grand Steak and Chop House in Des Moines when Drew Wright walked in.

"The usual?" Cunningham asked.

Wright pondered the offer. Brian made a great martini and it was sure tempting.

"No, it's primary day and I've got a lot of work to do tonight," he said. "I'll have an iced tea and the New York Strip, rare."

"Coming right up."

It was late afternoon, before the after-work crowd showed up at this preeminent cigar bar and eatery. The place was unusually quiet and was a nice respite from the craziness of the last few weeks. Not only was this an important race for governor but now there was a serial killer on the loose, knocking off candidates—or trying. Bob Blackwell was murdered. Then Carmelita Lopez. Someone had taken a shot at Louella Strong on the highway. Then there was that near miss that almost got Professor Vance at the Devonian Fossil Gorge in Coralville.

Jeez. Now it was a bi-partisan killer at work. What is normally a civilized campaign was turning very ugly and criminal. Not only were Iowans shocked, but the entire country was picking up on the story. Wright needed a break and a little food before election night began.

The reporter sipped on his tea and gazed at the television monitors above the bar. "Iowa is usually a place where they winnow presidential candidates," droned the Fox News anchor. "Now it's a place where gubernatorial candidates are winnowed by murder. Cameron Carlton has our report from Des Moines . . ."

Forget the normal issues of a campaign for governor. This was now a big national cop story. Media people were pouring into the state as if it were a caucus year.

Candidates were now traveling with state trooper and DCI bodyguard details. Iowa doesn't provide any kind of security for candidates, but the outgoing governor, Tom Vilsack, had used his executive authority to order some. The remaining candidates were grateful for the help, but placing them in security bubbles put a damper on the campaign. The President had even ordered federal investigators and agents into Iowa.

Every candidate was getting extraordinary press coverage everywhere, but it was deathwatch coverage. Got a candidate in your town? The local paper, TV, and radio stations were sure to be there—just in case.

It was downright spooky to go to campaign events anymore. Everyone in Iowa knew someone was out killing candidates for governor. That meant a lot of folks were staying away from rallies and events. No sense being in the line of fire. It also meant a lot of weirdos were starting to show up just to see if something more would happen.

The fun of an Iowa campaign was gone. Discussions of violence and gun control had replaced debates over education and the environment. What a sad state of events, Wright thought. You devote your life to covering politics and all of a sudden are back to your days as a police reporter.

"Here's your strip, Mr. Wright," Cunningham said. "And I threw in some asparagus too. Your mother would approve, and it's on that low-carb diet you're on."

"You're kind. I need a little TLC right now. How about a little wine with this, maybe a house meritage?"

"Coming right up," Cunningham said. "I didn't think you'd want to go through a primary night without a little something. Two glasses a day are good for the heart, you know."

"Does that mean four are twice as good for it?" Wright asked.

The voice at the end of the bar was familiar.

"Wright! How the hell are ya?"

"Well, Cameron Carlton," smiled Wright. "Welcome back to the prairie. At least you're back in June. Let's see, I'll bet Fox News is back to cover the Fourth of July celebrations. Maybe doing a preceed on the State Fair?"

Wright and Carlton had spent considerable time together during the last presidential campaign, prowling the back roads of Iowa, chasing candidates through snowstorms. Carlton was a good political reporter. He did his homework.

"Yeah, right," Carlton said as he pulled up a stool. "What is going on out here?"

"Crazy, isn't it," Wright said. "You had dinner? Brian, get this famished city boy some Iowa ethnic food. He needs some vittles before the polls close."

"Beef or pork?" asked Cunningham with a grin.

"I'll do the pork chop. Hash browns with cheese and the greens. Got any good local wines?"

Wright looked at his friend. "Uh, this is Iowa, Cam. The wine industry here is, shall we say, in its infancy. But Paul Tabor over near Baldwin has started up the Tabor Home winery and makes some decent reds. Why don't you bring us a bottle of the cab, Brian?"

"You got it."

Carlton scooted closer. "So, Wright, I hear you got a new job at the *Register* writing politics."

"Yeah, their guy quit to go to seminary. Mid-life crisis I guess. It's a good gig for me."

Carlton cut to the chase. "Is this a weird story or what? Gimme the lay of the land. Who dunnit?"

"Dunno. Blackwell was a guy who loved to fool around, so maybe his wife wanted him hit. But that doesn't explain everything else that's gone on since. Why these attacks on all the other candidates."

"Whose going to win tonight?"

"Dunno that either," Wright said. "Every time you get a cataclysmic event in a campaign—like Gary Hart dropping out because of an affair—the undecideds in polls go way up. It takes people time to decide where they want to land. The trouble with this campaign is that every time things start to settle down, someone takes aim at another candidate.

"The Republican polls have been up in the air. Lots of undecideds. After the Democrat, Vance, survived, his numbers bumped up, so I'd give him the edge there."

Cunningham brought the rest of the food.

"What do you think, Brian?" asked Wright. "Who is going to win? Whose the killer?"

"I'm betting on Vance to win the Democratic nomination," said Cunningham. "Who knows on the Republican side? You got me on the murderer question. It's about all anyone is talking about in here." Cunningham, like the other waiters in the state capital's top political eatery, was a political junkie and expert in his own right.

"I agree," Wright said. "I'll tell you, Cam, the waiters in here hear more political gossip in a day than you and I do in a week, so we'll defer to him."

The three shared a good laugh as the two dug in.

"Here's the Republican line-up," Wright said. "Louella Strong is a farm wife, but she's too much of a hothead for Republican business types. It's almost as if she belongs in the Democratic party. Same with Father Metterschmidt. I mean, a Republican priest? A lot of these Republican evangelicals would never vote for a priest. We don't want the Pope sitting in Terrace Hill. Lot's of folks like his moral tone, but they also aren't sure the clergy belongs on the campaign trail. But ever since the new Pope said it was okay for clergy to run for office again, I guess we'll be seeing more of this.

"Then there's Jim Taverus. He's a kook. Iowa's David Duke. Republicans may be conservatives in this state, even right-wingers, but this guy's an embarrassment. He likes guns and so do his people. Next time you're at one of his rallies, look at the bulges in the pockets.

"That brings up Ed Van Der Boomsma. He got in late after Blackwell was murdered, but he has a lot of the Republican money and power structure behind him. If he'd had more time, it would be a cinch for him, but the vote is still so fractured. You've got to get at least 35 percent of the vote in an Iowa primary to win a nomination and in a field this crowded, well, it's just hard to figure," Wright said.

"And if no one gets 35 percent?" asked Carlton.

"Then it goes to a state convention in mid-June. But that hasn't happened in this state since about 1960 when Jack Miller won a U.S. Senate nomination at a state convention."

"Got it," Carleton said. "What about the Democrats?"

"Vance. He's a bit of an egghead, but that gives him a nice base in Iowa City, Ames, and Cedar Falls. And look at the alternatives. Vance's being a widower has appeal. Labor's backing him. Vilsack's officially staying out of this, but his wife, Christie, is all for Vance. She's a better campaigner than Tom. She enjoys it. He puts up with it.

"Alan Fairfield is odd one. Keith Rolling is a gay vet. The Iowa Democratic party is pretty liberal, but it's not ready to nominate gay candidates just yet. Jeez, Cam, this is a state that has never elected a woman governor, senator, or U.S. House member.

"Now Winston Claridge is a big businessman. He and Louella ought to switch parties. No way the Democrats are going to nominate a business-type like that. Hey, Cam, it's just after 6. The afternoon exit polls will be in. Polls don't close until 9, but instead of all this speculating, let's go find out just who did win."

"You're on." ✣

✣ The two made the short stroll across the street to the Register. "There's good news tonight, Drew," said Randy Evans, the boss in charge on election night. "We have computers that are working."

"That's wonderful," Wright replied. "I hope you brought enough duct tape to keep them working. You know Cameron Carlton of Fox News? He's out for the big murder mystery."

Wright and Carleton sat down in front of the Voter News Service computer and punched in the password. The little green figures began to dance. On the Democratic side, the clear winner was Vance. He was projected to get about 55 percent of the vote. The Republican side was too close to call. No one was breaking 35 percent. Boomsma was in first, followed by Strong, then Metterschmidt—with Taverus way behind.

The VNS advisory said additional sampling was being done on the Republican side to try to come up with a winner, but it would be around 8:30 before anyone knew anything. The rules of the exit poll game are that no news organization is supposed to say who is winning or losing until the polls close. But those rules are being bent all the time and this year was no exception.

"It looks like a good night for Dr. Samuel Vance of Iowa City," intoned one broadcaster. "From Old Capitol to New Capitol, will the teacher be moving out of the classroom? We'll have full details coming up at 10."

The satellite vans began showing up outside the Hotel Fort Des Moines where Vance was having his victory party. Anyone who wants to know who is winning the network polls can watch the deployment of equipment and top anchors on election night—and here was more proof.

"Hey, Evans, this Republican thing is going to the wire," shouted Wright. "Could be a long night. We got somebody with every candidate?"

"Yes sir," came the reply. "But we pay you that big salary to tell us who is going to win."

"Yeah, and there's no way I'm going to give you a 'Dewey Wins' story as the hallmark of my journalism career," said Wright.

At 8:30, VNS posted the final exit poll numbers. Sure enough, no one got 35 percent. "No projection," flashed the screen.

"Looks like this Republican primary will go on for a couple more weeks until that state convention," Carlton said as he scrolled through the numbers on the screen. "Which one of the four wins at convention?"

"Boomsma would have the edge," said Wright. "But the convention doesn't have to pick from the list of candidates who ran. Now that they know Vance is the Democratic nominee, some will want someone else. At least we've got one nominee. What say we head over to the Fort to catch Vance's speech before I've got to file?" ✤

✤ Hotel owner Jeff Hunter normally wears a wry smile, like he knows something he won't tell you. Tonight he was frowning and quite willing to complain. The police had sealed off his hotel and everyone going in had to go through a mag detector.

"Mag detectors? I can't believe it," said Hunter. "This is usually reserved for presidential visits."

"Yeah, welcome to the campaign for governor of Iowa, 2002," said Wright. "If anyone does a big rally, the crowd all has to go through mag detectors first. For a while there they were getting lots of hits. It seems a lot of guys were showing up toting their piece. Gonna be Gary Cooper at high noon and return fire on the assassin. The mag detector really thins out a Taverus rally."

"That's incredible," Carlton said as he barked for a camera crew on his cell phone. The two waited in line with Hunter to clear the security check for the press. As they waited at the bottom of the stairs, Wright noticed a small group at the top carrying what appeared to be guitar cases. A bunch of scuzzballs with long hair and crosses hanging on their necks.

"I see you attract all kinds to your hotel, Jeff," said Wright.

"They're with the band. Showed up real early this afternoon before all the security people and the Vance people. They seem real laid back," said Hunter.

Wright was perplexed. Where had he seen that face before? And if they're with the band, who was in the hall right now belting out "Happy Days Are Here Again"?

DAVID YEPSEN *is* The Des Moines Register's *political editor. He is a native of Jefferson, Iowa. He holds a bachelor's degree from the University of Iowa and a master's degree in public adminstration from Drake University. In 1989 he was named a fellow in the press-politics center at the Kennedy School of Government at Harvard. He has covered Iowa politics for 25 years. He writes a weekly column, "On Capitol Hill," which appears every Monday. He is also a regular panelist on Iowa Public Television's* Iowa Press *program. He is married to Dr. Mary Stuart of Des Moines. They are parents of a daughter, Elizabeth.*

He has no plans to attend seminary.

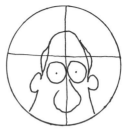

7.

Short-lived Victory

By O. Kay Henderson

The first time Drew Wright walked into the Hotel Fort Des Moines's Grand Ballroom, he was in high school and carrying his baritone case. The Iowa All-State Band was to practice in this room with its hardwood floor and extravagantly draped windows, and he'd earned a spot in the baritone section, in between the trombones and tubas.

Now, after more years than he cared to admit, he was in this room as a working reporter, cell phone in hand—and it was ringing.

"Where in God's name are you?" asked Randy Evans, the *Register* editor who was the paper's election night czar.

"I'm over at the Fort, waiting for a quick shot at Dr. Vance for the next edition, if you'll pardon the pun," Wright replied.

"You should be here in the newsroom, damn it. We've got someone there to catch quotes from his speech," Evans said.

Wright's stomach was in knots. He liked Evans, and he really needed this job after the tense months of trying to live the stringer's life, selling stories to publications for which the concept of prompt pay meant within the calendar year.

"I already re-worked the story from the first edition," Wright replied. The paper Iowans saw in Council Bluffs and Davenport was different from the one read by residents of Atlantic and Newton, a function of the time necessary to print the paper and get it trucked to the border areas.

Wright's second edition deadline was normally 9:30, but because it was election night, the deadline had been pushed back to 10:30 p.m.

"I've been promised a one-on-one with Vance before he speaks to the masses, and I'll get the quotes in the story for second edition," Wright said. "That way I'll be able to browbeat some usable quotes out of him rather than use the hash from his speech about how wonderful his supporters were."

"Where's your rewrite?" Evans asked.

"It's in the system," Wright replied.

As Evans mentally moved on to the next fire, he ended the conversation by hanging up, and Wright could hear the beginning of Evans's next conversation as the receiver was making its way from Evans's ear to his desk.

As Wright punched the "end" key on his cell phone, Arliss Harding, Vance's campaign manager, grasped his arm.

"To get into the holding room, you've got to be escorted by me," Harding said. The deaths of two of Iowa's 2002 gubernatorial candidates had prompted security akin to a president's, and the security presence was visible in the hotel.

Not only had reporters and guests been funneled through security checks, but police clad in their black uniforms and highway patrol troopers in their brown uniforms (sans hats) were stationed throughout the hotel, keeping their eyes peeled for sudden or suspicious behavior. A trooper was positioned at the door of the hotel's North Room where Vance's campaign staff had a holding area for their candidate. Dr. Vance, though, had been upstairs in one of the hotel's penthouse apartments for most of the afternoon, phone plastered to his ear, making last minute phone calls to get out the vote.

Vance had cast his own ballot in Iowa City at about 10:30 that morning, the perfect time to get TV shots that wound up on the noon hour newscasts. At about noon, Vance and a vanload of campaign workers had made their way to Des Moines, where Vance retreated to the hotel's 10th floor apartment which had served as a home away from home in the weeks before the primary, the perfect overnight stop as he campaigned in central and western Iowa. Jim Lightfoot of Shenandoah, the Republican gubernatorial candidate in 1998, had adopted "the Fort" as a second home during his bid for Terrace Hill. Fred Grandy, the Harvard-educated *Love Boat* actor-turned-politician, had used "the Fort" as home base, too, during his 1994 primary battle against incumbent Governor Terry Branstad.

When Wright arrived at the Fort with the Fox folks in tow, he had immediately pigeon-holed the Vance campaign manager about getting some time with the candidate as soon as possible.

"I've turned over tonight's scheduling to one of our campaign workers, Melissa Anchor," Harding had replied, looking around the room of milling campaign workers and supporters. "I don't see her. Here's her cell number. Call her and tell her we talked about putting you on the early list," Harding said as he scratched a seven-digit number on Wright's open notebook.

Wright removed his ever-present cell phone from his pocket and dialed. Anchor answered, and Wright could tell from the background noise they were in the same room but wouldn't be able to pick each other out of the crowd.

"This is Drew Wright, with the *Register*. I just talked to your campaign manager who said to tell you I need to be on the early list," Wright said. "I need to get some quotes to make it into second edition."

"O.K, O.K., you're on," Anchor replied. "You'll be in a small group going into the North Room at about 9:20 p.m."

"Where's the North Room?" Wright asked.

"It's on the north side of the ballroom. We decided to cordon it off rather than throw open the wall and extend the Grand Ball-room. The only access point is in the hallway, though, the hall-way where the men's room is."

"Thanks," Wright replied as he checked his watch and turned off his phone. Just a few minutes 'til show time. ✤

✤ By 9:25 Harding, in his new role as security escort, had as-sembled a small pack at the entrance of the North Room: a local TV reporter and her camera operator; the sports reporter from Radio Iowa, pulling election night duty with boom microphone in hand; an Associated Press reporter and photographer—and Wright.

"You don't have to check 'em," Harding told the Trooper. "I'll vouch."

The Trooper didn't reply and merely waived the group through to the center of the room where two maroon leather chairs sat on either side of a table which bore what Wright considered a gangly red, white and blue flower arrangement. The backdrop was a navy curtain, the same fabric that made the room's south wall. That would be the back of the press risers, Wright thought to himself. A tunnel of fabric was arranged so Vance could enter the north-west corner of the Grand Ballroom and shake hands down a rope line as he made his way to the stage for his victory speech.

Lights were already set for the TV crew, and Harding had the TV reporter sit in one of the chairs, a good shot for that "exclu-sive" Wright had hoped would be his alone.

The doors suddenly opened and Vance strode in the room with two more security escorts, his recently announced running mate Winston Claridge—and Claridge's dog. In the last two days Clar-idge had thrown his support to Vance in a deal that brought him the second-dog slot.

"Hello, good to see you," Vance said as he shook hands with the reporters. "What do you hear about turnout?"

Vance was dressed in a dark navy suit and a slightly lighter blue shirt with matching tie, the sort of *GQ* costume Regis Philbin wore during the heyday of that game show *Who Wants To Be A Millionaire?* It was not the traditional white shirt, red tie, dark suit look many politicians adopted.

The polite but stilted conversation concluded within a minute, and Vance took his seat. Suddenly the boxer, Winston, left his master's side, galloped over to Vance, and lay down at his feet.

"So much for canine loyalty," Wright chuckled to himself, "That dog has the instincts of a politician."

By 9:50, Wright was dialing on his cell phone again, calling Randy Evans at the *Register* to boast about the quotes he'd collected. Vance was dallying in the room with speech in hand, conferring with his campaign manager in hushed tones as the TV crew and the AP photographer hovered for more candid pictures. Wright had decided to make the call in this room as the din of music and conversation, which wafted in from the ballroom, was muted here.

"I've got the quotes. I'm on my way back to the newsroom," Wright said as he turned away from Vance.

Vance, meanwhile, tucked his notes into his suit pocket and bent to pet Winston one more photogenic time as Winston's owner, the defeated Democrat Claridge, inwardly seethed. The photographer had his TV camera on his shoulder with its light on, prepared to follow Vance for more video. His boss would like that last minute pet of the dog. He was glad he'd been rolling.

As Wright turned to leave the room, cell phone still at his ear, listening to a question from Evans, he heard a pop and immediately glanced toward Vance, who seemed to be buckling at the knees. To Wright, everything started to appear in slow motion: Vance's blue shirt splashed with a dark liquid that, from a distance, looked like soda pop, but was his own blood.

The navy curtain behind the risers swayed slightly, attracting his attention and that of the troopers. A shadow behind the curtain crumpled as a trooper's shot was fired. The dog was barking and barking and barking, licking Vance's face.

And the whole scene was being recorded by the two photographers.

"What's going on?" Evans barked into Wright's ear, drawing him back to real time.

"Vance was just shot," Wright said. ✤

✤ Although he should have been in the newsroom primary night, it was sometimes better to be lucky than good in the news business. Wright was able to dictate the story over his cell phone, and then linger at the crime scene as he knew one of the troopers from Governor Tom Vilsack's security detail who'd been assigned to Vance.

The photographers had gotten close-ups of Vance and of the shooter. The still photos were already being aired on the 24-hour news channels, for the AP photographer had downloaded his pictures via computer to the Associated Press wire. The local TV station was sharing its video with its network. Wright had dictated a first-person account that was to be featured on the *Register's* web site. And he had 10 minutes 'til his 10:30 deadline to rework his story.

The "perp" looked familiar to Wright, but he couldn't put a name with the face. Unkempt, shaggy hair, a cross. He'd noticed him at the top of the stairs with a guitar case when he came into the hotel earlier.

But he needed to focus on writing the biggest story of his career and he had a deadline.

(DES MOINES, IA) Another candidate in the harrowing race for Governor died Tuesday in a primary night shooting that felled

Dr. Samuel Vance on the day Iowa democrats selected him as their nominee.

Vance bent to pet Winston, the boxer dog and campaign companion of democrat Winston Claridge of Cedar Rapids, when he was struck by a bullet in the chest. He was preparing to enter the Hotel Fort Des Moines's Grand Ballroom to make his acceptance speech when he was shot.

"I love this state and I want to lead it to new horizons," Vance had told reporters moments before in an interview. "This murder mayhem is not going to deter me from my goals."

Vance, a retired University of Iowa professor, is the third gubernatorial candidate to be killed this year. Authorities have no suspects in custody for the murders of Robert Blackwell, the leading Republican candidate, and Carmelita Lopez, another GOP hopeful, but the gun authorities believe was used to shoot Vance was found near a man shot by a state trooper seconds after Vance was hit.

"We don't know his name. We don't know his motive," said Lt. Scott Dallas of the Iowa State Patrol. "He's in serious condition, and doctors won't let us interrogate him until he's been conscious and responsive for a few hours."

The suspect, clad in torn blue jeans, a tie-dye tee shirt and Army boots, was wearing a gold cross and carrying a guitar case earlier in the evening. A trooper on the scene returned fire in the direction of the shot which killed Vance. The suspect was found, wounded, underneath risers erected for the media covering Vance's primary night speech.

Wright quit reading the story. He'd written it, so he should know what it said. It was now 9:30 p.m. on Wednesday. Wright was at his desk in the newsroom, trying to tie up loose ends for the next wave of stories about the latest murder in a campaign that had turned politics in Iowa from deadly boring to just deadly.

It had been a whirlwind 24 hours, and he hadn't slept. Wright had stayed at the Hotel for hours, dogging the technicians gathering evidence, watching campaign workers and supporters for reactions. Investigators questioned him for only 20 minutes in their makeshift headquarters, ironically established in what was called the Governor's Room.

Wright reluctantly admitted to himself he wasn't much of a witness since he was looking the other way, talking on his cell phone, when Vance had been hit.

This afternoon's check with investigators had yielded an interesting tidbit: the bullet that killed Vance didn't match the one which killed Bob Blackwell in that park in Cedar Falls. Such quick ballistics work couldn't have been done in Iowa a few years ago, but could now thanks to the gizmo former candidate Jim Lightfoot had sold the state that month. Lightfoot now worked for a Canadian company, hawking a small, mobile ballistics test kit which was being used around the globe.

The suspect was still unconscious and seriously wounded. Wright got the impression there was a chance the guy would never wake up, but couldn't get a doctor to confirm it.

Another reporter stopped by his desk to get some feedback on the sidebar the *Register* was running on the Hotel Fort Des Moines. The Fort, built in 1919, had been host to nearly every President of the century. Woodrow Wilson was the first to stay at the Fort, followed by Harding, Coolidge, Hoover, Truman, Johnson, Nixon, Ford, Carter, and Reagan. Daddy Bush used the hotel during his campaign, and Clinton held meetings there in 1999. The hotel, which had earned a spot on the National Register of Historic Places, was now a place crawling with media and decorated with crime scene tape.

Now, both the Republicans and the Democrats would be choosing nominees at state conventions in June. One candidate, Democrat Keith Rolling, had told Wright in a phone conversation he was definitely not in the race. All the others who remained standing said they were campaigning for support among convention delegates.

In addition to the new information about the murder investigation, Wright had written a separate story about the intricacies of campaigning for the support of a select number of delegates as opposed to a primary vote. His campaign tactics story wasn't page one material, but was on the inside of the paper.

Despite a lack of sleep, Wright felt as if his body had an electrical current flowing through it—adrenaline, probably. He hadn't seen this sort of bustle around the newsroom since he'd taken the job. This was a story people wanted to read about, and in the crazy world that is journalism, the tragedy of a murder—the end of a once-famous life—morphed into a swirling vortex of information, pictures, and interviews that kept the 24 hour news machine humming.

By 2:30 a.m. on Thursday, Wright was ready to drive to his home in the Beaverdale neighborhood of Des Moines and crash. He'd learned by experience that once sleep was lost, it's lost forever. So, he set the alarm for 7:30, just five hours of sleep. ✤

✤ Wright woke up groggy, as expected, and made his way downstairs to his kitchen. He opened the refrigerator and looked at the contents—a month-old loaf of bread and beer—and shook his head. In the past month he could count on one hand the number of times he'd cooked for himself—and he'd have three fingers left over. If Wright was eating breakfast, he was going to order from a menu.

By 8:30, a freshly showered Wright was at the counter of the Waveland Cafe on University Avenue, ordering a sloppy breakfast of eggs, hash browns, bacon, and toast. Eating at places like the Wave was follow-through on his New Year's Resolution not to eat at franchise restaurants.

The coffee had already arrived, and he was spreading out an array of newsprint: *The New York Times*, *The Chicago Tribune*. Just a few papers to read for their take on the murder. Still disconcerted by the appearance of color photos in *The Times*, he absently gazed at the picture of Vance's shooter, and then froze mid-swallow. His mind had just clicked. That face. He'd seen that man in the park in Cedar Falls the day Blackwell had been shot.

O.KAY HENDERSON *is the news director of Radio Iowa, a statewide net-work serving 60 affiliated stations. Kay has been with the network since July 1, 1987, its first day on the air. She's sometimes seen as a contribut-ing reporter to the Iowa Public Television program* Iowa Press. *She grew up in Lenox, Iowa, and played baritone in the 1980 All-State Band. Her 1996 New Year's Resolution was to quit eating in franchise restaurants.*

8.
Call Her Louella

By Valerie M. Hudson

Louella Strong's solid, second place finish to Ed Van Der Boomsma in the Republican primary was the shot of political adrenaline she needed. The Strong campaign was operating on a shoestring budget, kept afloat lately with proceeds from bake sales and car washes. The candidate's inexperience and distaste for political fundraising had caused her to underestimate the need for big-dollar backers early on. "Strong for Governor" was on financial life support and it needed cash—fast.

Van Der Boomsma, the Pella farmer who replaced the late Bob Blackwell, had gained the support of big business with little effort. Early in the campaign, Mrs. Louella Strong railed against corporate hog lots; now Van Der Boomsma reeled in the corporate donors who saw her as a single-issue, anti-business candidate.

Some party leaders were embarrassed by her liberal leanings and there were jokes about trading her to the Democrats for Winston Claridge and a candidate to be named later. Homer McGruder, Van Der Boomsma's campaign manager, was quoted as saying Mrs. Strong had been watching too many reruns of *Maude*.

But this was no Maude Findlay. It was the new Louella, and Iowans were warming up to her. She had come a long way since her Memorial Day speech on the shores of Lake Okoboji. She was still outspoken about her vision for Iowa agriculture, but her message was more palatable once she softened the delivery.

Her speeches weren't the only things that had changed. At the urging of her family and advisors, she dropped the "Mrs." from her name and became a farmer.

She had always been proud of the title that came with her 1960 marriage to her high school sweetheart. She was Mrs. Louella Strong, the farm wife who brought her husband's dinners out to the fields, drove wagonloads of soybeans to the elevator, and clipped needle teeth at farrowing time.

A week after celebrating their silver wedding anniversary at a cake-and-punch reception in their church basement, Mrs. Louella Strong's husband died in a tractor rollover. The continued use of "Mrs." and "farm wife" was her tribute to their relationship, but over the years, it had faded to little more than a habit.

Her daughter-in-law was the one who suggested the candidate be known as, simply, Louella Strong. She argued that the marital status of the other candidates wasn't an issue and her mother-in-law's shouldn't be either. Besides, it sounded more modern.

During the same visit the two Strong sons suggested their mother adopt "farmer" as her occupation. After all, she'd had the responsibility of managing the 1,800-acre grain and hog operation since their father's death. Louella had proven she had exceptional business instincts, and she had made bold and progressive changes to the Century Farm. Still, that was no guarantee it would survive.

Louella Strong had spent long hours reflecting on the lives of family members who had worked, and died, on that farm. A picture of her great-grandparents hung in a heavy oval frame on her dining room wall. Her sons' high school graduation pictures were displayed below it. The generations were separated by time, and connected by land.

Louella had thought of them all when she first began to speak out on the future of Iowa's family farms. And she thought of them all when she finally announced her candidacy.

Yes, the metamorphosis of Louella Strong, farmer, was nearly complete and she emerged from the primary an invigorated, if broke, candidate. ✤

✤ "Mrs. Strong?" The reporter extended his hand as he introduced himself. "Drew Wright from *The Des Moines Register*."

"I know who you are, Drew, and call me Louella. It's a great day to be in North Iowa, isn't it?" she said as she ducked under his umbrella.

She had just come from a tour of the Park Inn Hotel, located across from Mason City's Central Park. Restoration of the architectural gem had begun two years ago, and Louella wanted to see for herself the progress that had been made.

"Drew, did you know this is the only remaining Frank Lloyd Wright-designed hotel in the world, and there were actually some people who didn't want to spend taxpayer money to save it?"

She turned around to take another look at the exterior of the building before moving on.

"Interested in Wright's work, are you?" the reporter asked.

"I'm interested in restoring and preserving Iowa's heritage, whether it's an old hotel, a hardware store on Main Street, or a family farm."

Several raindrops had fallen onto her wire-rimmed bifocals. She removed them and retrieved a clean, cotton handkerchief from her straw purse.

"See those DCI agents over there?" she whispered as she tipped her head to the right and gently wiped off the lenses. "I can't make any sudden moves without them getting all nervous. I'm not sure if they're here to protect me, or to try to catch me with a butcher knife in my purse."

Wright attributed Louella's dark humor to her uneasiness in the aftermath of Dr. Samuel Vance's murder. The mood on the campaign trail was somber, and after following that crackpot Taverus around yesterday, Wright welcomed the company of the sensible and sardonic Louella Strong.

The two DCI agents walked towards the candidate and she introduced Michelle Dean and Bill Haldeman to the reporter.

"Weren't you . . ." began Haldeman, as Wright's face began to register. Dean beat him to the punch.

"People's Park," she said.

"Guilty." Wright hadn't been on official business the afternoon those college kids stumbled onto Bob Blackwell's body. He thought he had been inconspicuous as he snooped around the crime scene, but obviously he wasn't the only one taking good notes that day.

The candidate was ready to move on.

"I'm heading for the Moose Lodge. Anyone care to join me?"

With that, Louella Strong covered her short, steel gray hair with her oversized purse and took off at a brisk clip down the street, sidestepping puddles so her new Naturalizers wouldn't get soaked.

The Red Cross volunteer at the registration table didn't recognize the candidate when she signed in. He smiled and handed her a clipboard and instructed her to fill out the form and read the attached information.

"This is nuts," thought Wright as he, Michelle Dean, and Bill Haldeman walked through the door behind Louella. Why would she take time out to give blood? What she needed to do was round up money and convention delegates.

The light rain had stopped and Haldeman went back outside while Dean and Wright sat down on metal folding chairs on either side of the candidate.

"What do you hear from the hospital?" Louella asked to no one in particular as she circled answers on the questionnaire.

"Nothing new. Still alive," Wright offered. They all knew the story of the most notorious patient in Iowa.

The suspected killer of the Democratic primary winner was a low-life named Rick Woodward. That was his last known alias anyway, according to the FBI's fingerprint database.

The trooper assigned to Vance's security that night at the Hotel Fort Des Moines brought down the suspect with a single round. The bullet ripped through Woodward's subclavian artery and he nearly bled to death before paramedics reached him.

He wasn't breathing on his own when he was wheeled into the emergency room, so doctors intubated him and placed him on a ventilator. Surgery repaired the damaged blood vessel, but he remained in the critical care unit—still "vented" and unresponsive.

Woodward, or whoever he was, had a rap sheet as long as an Iowa winter. His arrest record went back to his teenage years in New Jersey where he was picked up for petty theft, possession of drug paraphernalia, and gang activity. His left forearm still bore the purplish-blue tattoo of the gang's insignia, only the design was partially masked by a more recent tattoo of tiny flowers.

His criminal activity escalated after he dropped out of high school and an aggravated assault conviction in Illinois landed him in the correctional facility in Pontiac.

Special Agent Dean knew Woodward hadn't had any visitors, but a woman did call the hospital switchboard several times the night of Vance's murder. The operator told the DCI the caller sounded "anxious" when she asked about the suspect's condition. Each time she hung up before the operator could transfer the call.

Six days after Vance's murder, Rick Woodward remained under guard in the hospital, hovering somewhere between the afterlife and a life sentence. Should Woodward come out of his coma, there was some good news for him. Thanks to a young blonde nurse's assistant who was hired soon after he was admitted, he was clean-shaven and had a new haircut. Everyone agreed he looked pretty respectable—for an alleged assassin.

"How's my good friend Jim Taverus?" Louella flipped over the information sheet and kept reading as Wright laughed.

Wright didn't recall telling her he had been with her opponent yesterday. "He's fine. As full of hate as ever. Asked about you."

"Uh-huh. I bet he did."

She returned her questionnaire to the registration table and she and Wright moved up to the next row of chairs. Dean had stepped outside to speak with her partner.

The candidate set her purse on the floor and turned to the reporter.

"I'm more interested in your take on Father Metterschmidt. What's the deal with that guy?"

Louella was in the mood to shoot the breeze and Wright was ready to listen. She rarely held back her opinion about anything or anybody, but she expected you to cough up some good dirt, too, just to keep the conversation interesting.

She didn't give Wright time to offer any juicy tidbits on her Republican opponent. She was off and running.

"My daughter-in-law's Catholic and I thought I'd seen everything when the priest who married her and my son came riding up to the church on a Harley-Davidson. That's starting to look normal compared to the flaky stuff Metterschmidt does."

Dean returned to the waiting area.

"Who are we talking about?"

"Metterschmidt," the other two said in unison.

"I'd think you two would get along. He's for prayer in schools, peace, love and all that good stuff," Dean said. "Besides, what's not to like about a priest whose campaign slogan is "Violets Not Violence"?"

Louella rolled her eyes.

"Nothing strikes you as unusual about him? You don't think it's weird that he travels with his cat? I heard it belonged to the woman who lives in a little yellow house behind the rectory, but a priest with a cat named Violet? And don't you think that's a funny-looking cross he wears around his neck? It's not like any cross I've ever seen. Looks more like a Greek letter to me."

"Well, he is kinda cute." Dean couldn't believe those words came out of her mouth. Wright wished she hadn't said it, also.

"He does look a little like a young Richard Chamberlain," Louella said, throwing a rope into the hole Dean was trying to climb out of. "It's no wonder he's got women following him around. You know what they say, 'There is a charm about the forbidden that makes it unspeakably desirable'."

Dean saw that Wright was smiling.

"Which fallen politician said that?" he asked.

"It was Mark Twain. Now, if you two will excuse me, I've got lives to save." She followed a nurse behind a partition and left Dean and Wright to check their voice mail.

Louella came to the canteen area after her donation and was met by a volunteer who slapped a sticker on her lapel that read, "Be Nice to Me, I Gave Blood Today." The volunteer placed a glass of water on the table and asked if Louella would also like a doughnut and a cup of coffee.

"We used to just have cookies, but we found that we get a better turnout if we offer people the Krispy Kremes."

"Well, I'd better have one then. It'd be a shame to let them get stale."

The volunteer poured coffee for Dean and Wright, too.

"Do you ever worry that the next cup of coffee is poisoned, Louella?" asked the reporter. "Aren't you afraid to stay in the race?"

"What, and let the bad guys win?" she responded. "You know what real fear is, Drew? Fear is lying awake at 2:30 in the morning when your teenager was supposed to be home at midnight. Anyway, look around us. I bet half the so-called nurses in this room are State Troopers working undercover security. That's what I tell myself, anyway. That's how I get through it."

There was a commotion at the front door and everyone turned to see Winston Claridge, both the candidate and the canine, burst into the room.

Claridge had been in town and heard the Republicans had a candidate over at the bloodmobile. He grabbed a photographer and headed over to donate his own pint of compassion.

"Mrs. Strong, I didn't expect to see you here," he lied.

"It's Louella, please. Nice to see you, too."

Claridge looked around the room to see if all eyes were on him. They weren't, which disappointed him immensely. A Red Cross supervisor came over to tell him the dog would have to stay outside, so Claridge handed the boxer's leash to his aide.

"Don't tell them you're a Democrat or else they won't take your blood," Louella teased as Claridge went back to the registration table.

"Pathetic, isn't it?" she observed. She was eager to restart the conversation about the young, good-looking priest.

"Do you think voters really understand him? I may just be a meat and potatoes Methodist, but half the time I don't have a clue what he's talking about." She paused as she drank her coffee. "That must have been some monastery he lived in."

"Louella, is it true you call him 'Father Moonbeam'?"

"Maybe I have once or twice, but better 'Father Moonbeam' than 'Governor Moonbeam'." Louella wrapped the remaining half of her Krispy Kreme in a napkin and dropped it into her purse.

Winston Claridge's blood donation was not going well. He was lying on a cot with his feet elevated above his head and the nurses had him breathing into a paper bag to stop him hyperventilating. The photographer caught it all.

"One last thing about Father Metterschmidt, then I need to get going." Louella looked serious. "I think it's terrible he was nowhere to be found when poor Carmelita Lopez was dying at Lake Okoboji. Everybody knew Carmelita was Catholic, and I'm just saying that it would have been nice if she had received last rites."

Wright and Dean were still absorbing what they'd just heard as Louella shook hands with the volunteers on her way out the door. When they finally realized she'd left, they sprang from their seats to catch up with her.

As they raced down the sidewalk they passed Winston, who was swallowing the last of a half-eaten doughnut.

VALERIE M. HUDSON *is a free-lance writer whose observations about everyday life and popular culture have appeared in the* Mason City Globe-Gazette *since 1997. Her essays have also been published in* North Iowa Woman *magazine. She is a 3-gallon blood donor and an admirer of Frank Lloyd Wright architecture and Jan Karon books. She and her husband were married 22 years ago by a Harley-riding priest. They have two children and live in Mason City.*

9.

Dean's Day Off

By Pamela Briggs

Michelle Dean waited in line, buffeted gently by passersby, inhaling the clean, sweet aroma of butterfat-laden ice cream. She could almost taste it in the back of her mouth. There was no ice cream like this in Des Moines. She was going to pick up a couple of gallons of butter brickle, her mom's favorite.

Reflexively she scanned the area, identifying each type of person and noting them on a subconscious roster: shoppers, clerks, teens hanging out, mall walkers, here and there a security guard. Davenport's NorthPark Mall had changed a lot since she was a kid, but she could spot anomalies here as well as she could anywhere. Her innate knack for noticing things out of place, sharpened by years of training and fieldwork, was what made her lose her place in line.

It happened with an eerie kind of slow-motion rapidity. She saw every movement of the perp, every detail of the act and its aftermath, with utter clarity—but it unfolded so quickly there was no time to shout a warning: the toddler—clumsily wielding her scoop of melting chocolate ice cream in a cup cone, dripping it onto the tile; the man—leaving a store with a bulging plastic bag, eyes forward; his foot —coming down precisely on that slippery brown splotch, then skidding to the side, his legs splayed wide, off balance, arms flailing.

By the time he hit the floor Dean was crouching at his side. Did she obey this impulse because of her profession? Her compassion? Or because in one glance she'd assessed his physique as excellent and wanted to see if he had a face to match?

It couldn't be because she was worried about possible injury. His head hadn't hit the floor, and if he'd broken something he'd have been howling in pain, which he was not. Besides, she thought wryly, the only people in mortal peril these days seemed to be gubernatorial candidates, which he also was not. She pushed thoughts of work away. This was her weekend off.

She held out her hand. "Are you—" she began. The face which turned toward hers was Father Metterschmidt's.

"Brad Pitt? No, but I get that a lot," he said, grasping her hand warmly and springing to his feet. He quickly began gathering his scattered purchases. Dean shrugged off her shock and got up to help, surreptitiously looking him over. Same gold cross at his neck, same dimpled chin, same gray eyes. He was wearing a maroon Tee shirt (with white hairs clinging to it) and a very nice gold watch, neither of which she'd seen him wear before.

She handed Metterschmidt the last of the items he'd dropped— a fake beard and a mustache and a walkie-talkie. He was standing with his reloaded bag, looking down at the spot where he'd slipped. "Ice cream. Had to be chocolate. Figures. Stuff's determined to get me one way or another."

"Why? You on a diet?"

"Allergic. Even a taste of chocolate—any kind—gives me one hell of a migraine. You'd think they'd keep the floors cleaner here. I could sue."

"Actually, a little girl dropped it just as you were coming out of the store. I was in line at—"

"You'd also think people could manage to keep their precious darlings under control." Dean looked hard at him. Was this really Metterschmidt? The face was a match—the words weren't.

Could this be the man she'd heard speak on the sanctity of motherhood, the bonds of brotherhood, the blessings of family? He stepped closer. Though startled, she stood her ground. "I'm sorry. That sounded harsh. You're not a mother, are you?"

Dean fought to keep defensiveness out of her tone, and lost. "No, but I have one. Actually, it's her birthday today."

"Oh, isn't that nice," he said, instantly making her feel like a babbling kindergartner. What was it about this man that made her feel so tongue-tied and awkward, for heaven's sake?"

On second thought, she knew exactly what it was.

But was he who she thought he was? Why wasn't he acting the eager, idealistic candidate, especially in front of her? Could it be that he didn't recognize her? They'd both been at Lake Okoboji only a couple of weeks before. Dean was used to drawing attention at times while doing her job, and nothing commands attention like giving CPR to a drowned woman in the middle of a crowd. Or did he recognize her and was affecting this persona, hoping she wouldn't realize it was he?

This was all too much to take in on what was supposed to be her weekend off.

Her cell phone burbled. She glanced at the Caller ID display. Bill. She wasn't expecting him to call, so it had to be important. She couldn't take the call in front of Metterschmidt—maybe he really didn't recognize her, and she didn't want him to at this point. Excusing herself and answering would be conspicuous. But ignoring the ringing would be worse. Maybe the sound would be lost in the babble of the mall.

As she was reaching for the phone, it stopped ringing. That problem was out of the way, for now at least. She'd call Bill as soon as she could.

"I'm sorry. I've been a bit short with you," Metterschmidt was saying. "Taking a tumble like that in public puts me off my feed, and I was just buying gifts for my nephew's birthday. Can I buy you some coffee? Or a beer?"

It had been awhile since someone had made such an offer to her—and the last time, she had felt no attraction. This time, the attraction was there. Since it was only physical, however, she could answer him easily and honestly, suppressing the shock of being asked out by a priest. "Oh, I appreciate it, but no thanks. I've got to get my ice cream home to my family before it melts."

"You don't have any ice cream."

The awkwardness hit again, and again she felt her face get warm. "Right. I was in line. Never got to the counter. I should have said, 'I've got to get in line to get my ice cream and then get it home before it melts'." Now she was babbling.

"Hey, you gave up your place in line to come to my rescue and I didn't even thank you." Was that friendly bantering, or was she hearing sarcastic mock-gratitude in his tone? "Thank you. And you are?"

"Mi—Michelle." She'd nearly given him the name her friends called her. She held out her hand again, and he grasped it strongly. His hand was very warm.

"Phil."

"Nice to meet you. I've got to get in line for that ice cream now. Watch your step."

"I will now."

She got in line and watched him stride away. Slipping her 35-millimeter from her bag, she clicked off a few shots. Photos of him from behind would be better than nothing. While waiting, she replayed the encounter in her mind, letting the details soak in. As she was paying for her ice cream, her phone rang. Bill again, calling when her hands were full, naturally. She dropped her change, picked it up, grabbed the paper bag, nearly dropped that, left the counter, and answered the phone, pushing past a crowd of teenagers.

"Yeah?"

"Hey Mick, what do you think?"

"Nothing, really. The Fates seem to be conspiring to deprive me of ice cream. What's up?"

"Listen to this. I was talking with my dad. He thought 'Metterschmidt' was a weird name—and his mother was German. He mentioned that 'Messerschmitts'—that's two s's instead of two t's—were a type of German bomber in World War II. So I got curious and started checking. There are no Metterschmidts in any Iowa phone book I can find."

"All right. He's from here. I'll look him up for you. But don't we have his number on file?"

"That's not the point. And what do you mean, 'from here'? He's from Davenport."

"I'm in Davenport."

"What are you doing in Davenport?"

Dean winced and pulled the phone away from her ear briefly.

"It's my mom's birthday. What's the problem? And what's your point about the phone books?"

"The point is, the name doesn't seem to exist. Anywhere. I couldn't even find it on the entire Web."

"So it's an alias?"

"Not exactly. I've been calling around to libraries and one of them has *The Catholic Messenger* indexed. They faxed me a short article that mentions him."

"So great. So he exists."

"Yeah, Metterschmidt exists. Or used to. But that might not have much to do with our young Richard Chamberlain candidate."

"Brad Pitt," she corrected absently.

"What?"

"Never mind. Go on."

"Mick, there's a photo with this article. And this Metterschmidt looks like Gomer Pyle. An overweight Gomer Pyle at that."

"So they misidentified him in the caption."

"Possible."

"Anyone else in the photo who could be our Metterschmidt?"

"No way."

"What year was it taken?"

"Uh, let me see—1996."

"So he lost weight and got a good haircut."

"Trust me—it can't be. Unlike the guy we've been calling 'Metterschmidt,' the one in the paper has a huge Adam's apple and does not have that cute little John Travolta thing in his chin."

She smiled at his slightly petulant tone, then lost the smile when he said, "Why don't you want to believe this? Do you know something I don't?"

She did, of course, and it actually fit with Bill's information. Why was she reluctant to tell? She almost felt guilty. "Actually, I was at the mall—still am—and guess who fell on his face right in front of me?"

A pause. "You're joking."

"Then he trashed mothers and babies. Said 'hell.' And he came—came on to me."

"What?"

"I think."

"Tell me. From the top."

She told him, in detail and as objectively as possible.

"Mick, that makes my skin crawl. The whole thing. His behavior with you, and the fact that while I was calling you he was standing right in front of you—"

"I know." Despite her efforts to keep her account straightforward, Bill had picked up on her feelings—or maybe was having skin-crawling feelings of his own about Metterschmidt. They had that knack in common. "Now what?"

"I'm waiting for the Diocese to fax me some information about the priest, whoever he is, or was. Records of his schooling, where he was assigned when, what he was supposed to be doing. And they're looking for more photos."

"Fax it all on to me. And fax what you've got now."

"Yeah. Where?"

"Hold on. I'll get you a number." She had been walking the mall while talking instead of going out to her car. Walking with the phone gave her privacy. Also, she felt safer inside with people around than she would have outside in the parking lot, exposed—although being in crowds hadn't helped any of the murdered candidates.

She stopped by a phone kiosk and found the number for Kinko's. As she put her receiver to her ear again, she noticed a couple walking past, both around her age. The woman touched the man's face, and their melodious laughter mingled and rose above the Muzak and the other crowd noises. The man stroked the woman's long hair. Dean was astonished to feel tears in her eyes and blinked them away. She could indulge in self-pity later. Now she was on duty; this wasn't her weekend off anymore. She gave Bill the number.

"Oh, and another thing," he said. "I've been looking at photos and Louella Strong was right. It's not a cross he's got; it's a tau. The Greek letter."

Dean consulted her recent mental picture of Metterschmidt and nodded. "Yeah, the jump ring at the top could fool you into thinking it's a traditional cross. So he was in a fraternity?"

"I don't know. Frat names have three letters, of course. But I researched it."

"Yeah, nice *seat*work, I'm sure." She couldn't resist her traditional jibe at Bill's fondness for Internet research. Just like legwork, only sitting down.

"The tau has mystical significance in a lot of cultures: for Catholics, Protestants, Hindus, ancient Egyptians, ancient Central Americans, and ancient Greeks of course. Listen to this. Tau means, 'You will have a parting from the companions around you.' It's said to mean either a welcome release from enemies or an unwelcome parting from friends."

Dean let this sink in. "Speaking of departures, any news on Woodward?"

"Still circling the drain."

She sighed. "All right. Anything yet on the latent prints taken from Blackwell?"

"Still waiting. Oh, and I also found out tau means 'rope' in German."

"So?"

"So nothing. It's interesting."

"Call me when you know more. I've got to get to Kinko's and over to Mom's before this ice cream completely melts."

"Tell her happy birthday for me. I'm sorry to call you on your day off."

"No, you're not, and neither am I. I would've called you anyway about Metterschmidt—or whoever he is."

"You don't sound good."

She sighed. "I don't know, Bill. Something about being home, and at this mall, just makes me feel like a kid again. Not necessarily in a good way. I'm upset with myself about that whole Metterschmidt thing. I should have handled it better."

"Listen, you were taken off guard and you were cool. You got information for us, got some photos, and didn't tip your hand."

"But how could he not have known who I was?"

"You've got some ego on you."

"All right. Thanks. Talk to you later."

"Yeah. Bye."

Dean put her phone away and finally headed for the parking lot, remembering Metterschmidt's response to her goodbye. She had said, Watch your step. He had replied, I will now.

PAMELA BRIGGS *was born and raised in Davenport. She writes contemporary fantasy, horror, erotica, and nonfiction, and works at a public library. Aside from voting, her sole political involvement has consisted of singing with an a cappella quartet at a fundraiser luncheon for a Democratic senatorial candidate (who subsequently won). Her website is at http://www.deconstruction-zone.net*

10.

The True Believer

By Dennis Goldford

Samuel Orestes Blowhard does the 1-4 p.m. shift at WHAT radio (666 on the AM dial). People always liked the station's billboards advertising the show: "Beware of imitators! Tune in to the real SOB on WHAT." This was 50,000 clear-channel watts of half-truths and distortions, preying on the less than fully informed minds of his (mostly male) listeners.

The company that owned WHAT made a lot of money from the station, not that it needed any more than the fortune it had already made with its schools of phrenology, but it wanted to balance its reputation for broadcasting one-sided, highly partisan fare. It therefore donated a ton of money to a small school in central Iowa, Peripheral College, on the outskirts of Pella. Peripheral had been around for quite a number of years, but it had never participated in the life of the town. Now, however, thanks to WHAT, it had its own Institute for Political Analysis, headed by the esteemed Bat Guano, who held the Blowhard Chair.

Guano, born in New Jersey as Battista Guanoliotta, had come to Iowa in the mid-1980's and soon appeared regularly as a political commentator on television. Drew Wright had often called him for perspective in the past, but when Guano would not agree with one of Wright's story lines, Wright began to rely on a retired professor from Faber College in Lost Nation. He had a fond memory of Lost Nation, having dated a woman from there who put the P in "party," and so he enjoyed the familiarity of calling that old local telephone exchange. At the same time that memory was tinged with a little sadness, even for a gruff guy like himself. He had thought of getting serious with this woman, but when her family objected ("What kind of a life would a woman have as the wife of a reporter?"), she ended the relationship in the words of the old Barbara Mandrell song: "If lovin' you is wrong, I don't wanna be Wright." That really hurt. ✤

✤ Guano was at work on a difficult problem: he was trying to explain how the same state could elect both Tom Harkin and Charles Grassley to the U.S. Senate. Reporters and everyday citizens alike had asked him this question ever since he arrived in Iowa, and he finally found it tó be such an idiosyncratic, if not irrational, phenomenon that he decided to devote substantial attention to solving the riddle. The solution continued to escape him, and he was coming close to concluding it was just one of those things we're not meant to understand.

The murders in the current gubernatorial campaign thus came as a welcome diversion for Guano, giving him the opportunity to justify putting the Harkin-Grassley conundrum aside for a while.

"This assassination business isn't politics," he thought to himself in the post-primary days leading up to the state convention. "It's *The Godfather* on the prairie—except that instead of a meal of pasta and wine, we get a meal of beef and noodles over mashed potatoes with gravy and corn, and a glass of milk." His New Jersey heritage made him chuckle. No oregano or garlic for these sturdy citizens—in Iowa ketchup and mayonnaise count as spices! And there's enough starch on one plate of this cuisine to crease the burial clothes of a dozen dead gubernatorial candidates for a long time.

Guano took a lot of heat for his analyses, such as his recent commentary called "The Weaknesses of Louella Strong," or his uncovering of Keith Rolling's involvement with Big Tobacco in a series Guano called "The Rolling Papers," or his exposé of Alan Fairfield's private idiosyncrasies entitled "Strawberry Fairfield Forever." But while Republicans distrusted Guano as a closet Democrat, and Democrats distrusted him as a closet Republican, the general public accepted him as a neutral, fair-minded if tough analyst. He always said that on election night the television anchors did the play-by-play while he was the color commentator, trying to put events and issues into perspective and context for the average person. "You have to assume that your audience is intelligent but uninformed," he explained, "whereas with politicians you simply know that they're informed but unintelligent."

Guano was contemplating looking into the involvement of Catherine Shark and two of her cousins, Pool and Loan, in a trained water-creature entertainment business, in a report tentatively titled "Catherine Shark: Woman with a Porpoise," when the phone rang.

"Bat? Drew Wright here. If you have a moment I'd like to talk to you about your perspective on this killing season we seem to be having in the race for governor."

Even if Wright didn't call as much as he used to, Guano enjoyed talking to him. The difference between television and newspaper coverage of politics was interesting, one Guano hadn't recognized until he began to appear in both media. Television, of course, is a highly visual medium, and it covers people and events well. As awful as it sounds, nothing makes for great television like a catastrophe, such as the Challenger disaster or Jack Ruby's shooting of Lee Harvey Oswald right in front of the cameras. (Indeed, that memory was tempting Guano to state publicly that the Iowa State Patrol was in danger of qualifying for the

Dallas Police Department award for outstanding protection of a public figure.) The last thing in the world television wants is an hour of "talking heads."

Newspapers, on the other hand, cover issues and institutions well, Guano had determined. The problem with newspapers is that most people get their news—what news they bother to get—from television. Guano liked the chance to take the time to get into an issue in depth with a newspaper reporter, even if the reporter was going to use only a line or two, the newspaper equivalent of a TV or radio sound bite. As he learned during several Iowa caucus cycles, the newspaper folks usually wanted a good background as context when dealing with a particular story, and Guano was more than happy to help educate them when he could. On the other hand, he liked the chance TV offered to reach a much wider audience, even if television reporters generally didn't know politics and government as well as newspaper reporters. However, in Iowa Guano felt fortunate to work with some sharp television people whose coverage he respected.

"So, Drew, what do you need?"

"Bat, this is just crazy, and I've seen crazy in my time. What do you make of it?"

Guano paused, choosing his words carefully. "Drew, this is tough for me. I'm used to dealing with politics in terms of general factors like voter turnout, campaign dynamics and funding, political advertising, and the like. This business now, all these murders, is a matter not of general trends but of particular, real, live people. A cop and a psychiatrist might do a better job for you here than I can."

"Yeah, I know, Bat," Wright said. "But to identify suspects we need to look for motives, and you might be able to help throw some light on who has what to gain and lose politically by these murders."

"Well," said Guano, "before I even consider the political side here, I'd venture the thought that the killer—or killers—could be working from two types of motive. One would be what I'd call personal ambition or revenge—you know, someone who either had a grudge against the victims or saw them as standing in the way of the person he supported."

"Okay, Bat, I'll work on the personal side with other people, but tell me what your second type of motive is."

"I don't have a fancy name for this one, Drew, but I guess I'd look at the factor of political, as distinct from personal, ambition or revenge. We can understand the guy acting out of personal reasons, whether for money, revenge, jealousy, and so forth, but this second case I'm thinking about involves the kind of political ideologue—the true believer—that we've seen throughout history. Maybe this sounds far-fetched for good old salt-of-the-earth Iowa, but for the past 35 or 40 years in American politics we've seen a lot more of these true believers. These are the guys—or women, of course—who are so convinced of the truth, with a capital 'T,' and the virtue of their views that people who oppose those views aren't just their opponents. People who differ with them are, in their eyes, their enemies. For the true believer, politics is a kind of warfare. In fact, a neat little reversal just occurs to me. Do you recall the famous saying of von Clausewitz that war is just politics by other means? Most normal, everyday people would probably agree with that. Well, perhaps what I'm trying to say here is that for the true believer politics is just war by other means."

"This is getting a lot deeper than I wanted," Wright complained, "but I have to admit that it's interesting. Tell me more—but remember that I'm a reporter with a deadline."

"Yeah, yeah—take it out of that mythical check your editor's going to send me!"

"Okay, okay, I know you're doing me a favor. So do it," Wright replied.

"Here I go, getting philosophical again," Guano agreed, "but what can I say? I'm an academic. It's my occupational hazard.

"Okay, okay. Back to the true believers."

"All right," Guano agreed, "but let me have the space to lay out my point. Politics, as we political scientists like to say, is the process by which people negotiate their differences. It's the old Rodney King question: 'Can't we all just get along?' In other words, in any society you have an ineradicable diversity of people, people with all sorts of values and beliefs that don't always fit together harmoniously. Still with me?"

"Yeah, wise one," Wright replied. "I'm not as dumb as I look."

"You couldn't be."

"Okay, you got me. Now back to the topic."

"Well," Guano continued, "the problem is how people of different and often conflicting values can live together in the same society. Politics involves agreeing to disagree."

"So far, so good," Wright noted, "but get to the point."

"I'm getting there. Agreeing to disagree means that we accept the legitimacy of difference. In other words, people have to be allowed the right to be wrong. Violence, like these murders, however, if it's for political rather than personal reasons, indicates that someone out there has the view that people do not have the right to be wrong. It's the ideologue, the true believer, who's most capable of political violence because he's so convinced that only he possesses Truth and Virtue that anyone holding views to the contrary cannot be merely different, but, rather, must be wrong and sinful. For the true believer, error has no rights; sin has no rights."

Wright hadn't stopped his note-taking. "Are you saying the killer has to be some sort of fanatic?"

"Sort of," Guano replied, "but I want to try to be clear about what I'm suggesting. You know the old phrase, 'The only things certain in life are death and taxes.' Taxes aside, death is certain not only in that it's going to come, but also in that it's irreversible. It's absolute: once it's done, it's done. The average person has enough skepticism about his own knowledge that, at least in most matters, he can say, 'But I might be wrong.' The true believer, though, is possessed of absolute certainty: I'm right. I'm virtuous. My enemies are wrong and evil—and cannot be allowed to go their errant ways."

"C'mon professor," Wright said impatiently, "let's fish or cut bait. What are you telling me here?"

"Okay, Drew here it is. These murders could well be committed by an unbalanced person, or by someone with strictly personal motives of ambition or revenge. I can't help you there as to possible suspects. But political murders, murders done for political, as opposed to personal, reasons—especially murders committed for a cause, a so-called greater good, rather than merely for a job—are committed by true believers. So look to see if there are any potential true believers among your suspects. A true believer can be a religious person who has forgotten that he is not God, or he can be a political ideologue who sees himself as serving the master race, or the revolutionary class, or history, or the reign of virtue. But bear in mind that the most effective true believer is not the apparently raving lunatic. It's the guy so totally convinced of his own wisdom and virtue that he's totally at peace with himself."

"So, I don't have to look for fangs?"

"No, Drew—at least if you're not looking at your journalistic rivals. Your most effective true believer looks just like a normal person—even an apparently warm, good-humored person. He just lives in a completely alternative mental and moral universe."

"Bat, you've worn my ear off. I'm glad we don't pay for local calls by the minute," Wright said.

"Hey—last time I checked the *Register's* papa, Gannett, has VERY deep pockets."

"You'd have to check with the guys upstairs about that," Wright said. "But you're telling me, then, to look for the person, no matter how charming and sympathetic he might appear, who's so convinced of his absolutes that he's willing to wield the absolute, irreversible weapon—murder—in service of them. Right?"

"Right. Unless this really is some sort of personal grudge match. With my luck it'll turn out to be the Terrace Hill housekeeper who's tired of cleaning up after the governors! In any case, Drew, you owe me a major beer—and I don't mean domestic."

"I'd better make it a full case, then, because I have one more topic to raise with you."

"I'll bet I know what it is," said Guano. "Maybe a little normal politics—'conventional' politics, as it were?"

"Yeah," replied a tired Wright. "While I've got you I should get your thoughts on the results of the state conventions this past weekend."

"I figured you were coming to that at some point," said Guano.

"Okay, Bat, let's take the Republicans first. Were you surprised?"

"Yes and no. I'm not surprised they nominated Van Der Boomsma. Not only did he finish first in the primary, but his background as a farmer from Pella, a businessman, and a regular four-square relatively parochial Iowan fits the party. You have to remember the four basic legs of support for the Republican Party of Iowa. They are the rural vote, the elderly vote, the business vote, and the Christian-conservative vote. Van Der Boomsma fits quite comfortably, if unexcitingly, on all four of those legs."

"Yeah," Wright agreed, "unless he says or does something completely off the wall, covering him is going to be worse than watching paint dry."

"The surprising aspect of the convention, however, was Van Der Boomsma's getting Louella Strong to agree to run as his Lt. Governor. Iowans do not seem quite ready for a female governor, but, as I would suggest about a female president as well,

I tend to think the first female chief executive is likely to be a Republican rather than a Democrat, because if she were a Democrat, the Republicans would tar her as a radical, bra-burning Evita. Being a Republican woman will neutralize that issue for all but the most retrograde types."

"And Louella may activate a constituency among independents—who still have a plurality in the voter-registration totals—and even some Democrats who would vote for the ticket even if she's not at the top, I would guess."

"Yes, we might call that the Liddy Dole effect, in honor of the excitement Mrs. Viagra stirred up here in Iowa in 1999."

"Okay, Bat, so that's the Republican ticket, but what about the also-rans?"

"Taverus is probably off to a Klan meeting, or some such beyond-the-fringe event. But Father Metterschmidt is more interesting here. Word has it that he's going to denounce the convention, and especially the pairing of Van Der Boomsma and Strong, as proof that the party is corrupt. If he wants to stay in the race, though, he's got a problem. It would take too much time and effort to try to get on the November ballot by petition, not to mention the problems a write-in candidate would face. But I can give you a hunch, if you want."

"Go ahead," Wright said. "What can he do?"

"My guess, which, again, is only a hunch at this point, is that he could try to pull a Pat Buchanan. Good ol' Pat jumped from the Republican Party to the Reform Party back in 2000, mostly because of that $12.5 million in matching funds available because of the Perot campaigns in 1992 and 1996. With Perot quiet during 2000, you'll recall, the Reform party basically suffered a meltdown, with Buchanan allying with, of all people, the Marxist, black nationalist Lenora Fulani. Talk about strange bedfellows!"

"Yeah, that was nuts. Pat's getting into bed with Lenora is screwing everyone else. But how does that fit in with Metterschmidt?"

"Well, remember—the Reform Party had been silent on social issues, and Buchanan and his supporters split the party, with Jesse Ventura and others bailing out when they imposed their hard-edged social agenda on the Reform Party platform.

"Buchanan left the Republicans, but he never left his hard-line anti-abortion, anti-homosexual, pro-school-prayer agenda. I'm not sure how far Metterschmidt would go down this road—he's been pretty non-committal thus far—but my point is that the Reform party nomination would give him the ballot line he needs to compete in the November election. The petition and write-in routes just won't give it to him."

Wright was impressed. "Very intriguing. I don't believe I would have thought of that. You're a credit to your Italian countryman, Machiavelli."

"Yeah—maybe since he wrote *The Prince* I should write *The Priest*. Just remember that this is all a hunch at this point, but one that seems to make the most sense given the legal requirements and the political lay of the land at the moment."

"Okay, then, let's take a quick look at the Democrats. Why in the world did they nominate Claridge? He's not the brightest guy in the world."

"Well, for one thing, remember that 'bright' doesn't necessarily make for the most effective chief executive. Remember Carter and Reagan, for example. But I think that the nomination of Claridge signals the thinness of the Democratic bench. With Vilsack dropping out, and Vance having been dropped out, so to speak, there's just not a lot of talent of state-wide stature for the Democrats right now. Chet Culver is probably interested at some point, but he's still awfully young."

"So are the Democrats conceding this race, sending in Claridge just to hold the place on the ballot while they concentrate on the statehouse races?"

"I think 'conceding' might be a bit too strong at this point, though I see why you use that word. But consider also that Claridge's background as a businessman in Cedar Rapids, particularly with his computer focus, might well soften the hard union edge the Democratic Party wears in Iowa. Independents who are unimpressed with Van Der Boomsma and unwilling to support the ticket because of Louella might well see Claridge's business background as a bit of an antidote, or at least a protective shield, against the IOU the unions might issue a successful Democratic candidate."

"But is Claridge the best they've got? What about the other candidates—presuming, as we speak, that they're still alive."

"Yeah, this is a dangerous business, isn't it? Barring a 'white knight,' a viable and attractive someone who rides in and convinces Van Der Boomsma to surrender the nomination, all the Democrats have is Fairfield, Rolling, and Shark. If Iowans aren't ready to elect a woman, especially a Democratic woman, to Terrace Hill, they sure as hell are NOT going to elect either Fairfield or Rolling, with their personal proclivities. And, while Shark has won a few minor, local races, when it comes to the governor's job Iowans are still so parochial that Branstad and Lightfoot, in their races, could insinuate that Campbell and Vilsack, respectively, were not fit to be elected because they weren't born in Iowa. Vilsack did make it, of course, partly because Lightfoot was so uninspiring even to moderate Republicans, but also because in his years here Vilsack has taken on the mild, modest personality Iowans seem to like. Catherine Shark, a New Jersey transplant like me (except that I'm not running for anything), is just too abrasive for Merle and Ethel in Jefferson or What Cheer."

"So we're left with Claridge"

"Yeah, but we can hope his dog gives him good campaign advice."

Wright sighed. "Bat, I'm exhausted, and I imagine you are too.

Thanks so much for the perspective on all of this stuff. I may go back to doing movie reviews if I survive reporting this campaign."

"Drew, I envy you that luxury. I still have to figure out how Iowans can send both Harkin and Grassley to the U. S. Senate. Maybe working on cold fusion would be easier."

DENNIS GOLDFORD *is Associate Professor and Chair in the Department of Politics and International Relations at Drake University where he teaches American politics and political and constitutional theory. This is his first excursion into fiction writing, and he has not missed the apparatus of footnotes and bibliography at all.*

11.

All That Jazz

By Stephanie Keenan

July in Iowa features gnats, mosquitoes, 90 degree temperatures, 95% humidity, and "The Bix." Other towns in the middle of the Midwest hold quaint commemorations honoring their favorite sons and daughters too. But none get as excited or sweaty as Quad Citians when they laud Bix Beiderbeck, musician and horn player extraordinaire, a man who died in his twenties of booze and drugs and too much high life. Yes sir, in this man's honor the streets of Davenport fill with street vendors selling everything from sweet corn on a stick to statuary depicting crows and grasshoppers made with farm tools. Hot and cool jazz wails from the riverfront and the population swells to a great big old horde.

Early on the second to last Saturday of July, thousands of world class, and those who wanted to brag they ran with the best, packed the bottom of Brady Street hill in anticipation of the Bix Run, a grueling 7 mile march up and down the wannabe San Francisco streets in weather only good for growing corn.

Normally held on the last weekend in July, this year the Bixers lost out to the golfers at the John Deere Classic. After all, in the Quads, nobody runs things like the Deere.

Joan Benoit Samuelson and Billy Rodgers were there in per-

son and in bronze. However, Kenyans generally win the race because they are used to the hills, heat, and humidity. They wind
up taking the $10,000 purse and the new car.

So, with more people gathered in one place than anywhere else
in Iowa at this time of year, the gubernatorial candidates flocked
in along with half the state's population, especially the ones who
loved the nightly jazz concerts held on the levee under the watch-
ful eye of *The Rhythm City* riverboat, one of two on the Iowa side.

Michelle Dean tucked a strand of hair back under her sweatband and felt her muscles scream as she headed up Kirkwood
Boulevard on the last of the Bix practice runs. Glancing around,
she saw her partner, Bill Haldeman, trip and belly flop onto the
asphalt. She reversed course as several fellow practicers stopped
to give their fallen comrade aid. By the time she got there Bill
had been helped to a lawn and was sitting up, telling the people
surrounding him he was okay.

"Hey, Grace," she said, skidding to a stop in front of him. She
couldn't stop the laughter that bubbled up as she surveyed the
damage. Haldeman's nose, one of the larger, more patrician
noses in the special agent business, seemed to be a bit mushed
and skinless on the slope. Both knees were scraped and the el-
bows and hands repeated the theme. He looked like a half-
plucked chicken, ruffled feathers and all.

"Thanks a bunch, Agent 10 and 1/2. Like I laughed when you
were almost run down by that truck in West Branch, or when that
marijuana ditch grower blasted you with pellets . . ."

"Yeah, you did. I remember when they had me face down on
the gurney, my bottom full of more buckshot than it would take
to bring down a fully racked deer, and you spanked my derriére
while hee-hawing outrageously as they wheeled me away."

"And *I've* never been hurt before? If you want to get into com-
paring scars . . . ." He winced as he touched a blood-pocked hand
to his nose which was spurting blood in sync with the pulse of a

sprinkler behind him.

Michelle reached into her fanny pack and pulled out some tissues that she then rinsed in the spraying water, and, tilting his head back, placed the soggy mess over the bridge of his nose, pinching slightly.

"Ouch, Oooch, damn, Mick, you trying to kill me?"

Keeping her grip on the nose, she wiggled it slightly. "It doesn't feel like it's broken," she screamed above his squealing. "Just stop now. You sound like a pig getting its privates snipped off."

Bill shivered and said some not-for-use-in-mixed-company phrases, then plopped onto his back. "Tell me again," he nasaled, "why we're racing up and down hills that a goat wouldn't touch?"

Dean, not wanting to break her race rhythm completely, jogged around his prone form. "Because we're elected to protect the almost elected, and two of them are going to run, in the 7 mile race, that is."

"Stop bouncing around; you're making me queasy," he moaned. "Have you decided who you're going to tail?"

"I said I'd let you decide."

"Well, since I've just lost the outer layer of my skin and suffered acute blood loss, I don't know if I can even keep up with Louella Strong."

"So, you think you'd have trouble with a gray-haired widow, mother of two grown children, a woman of a certain age?"

"We've both had trouble keeping up with her, and you know it. Plus, I'd better take on the good Father or whoever he is. You're liable to trip on your drool if you do it."

"I don't think I'll even dignify that with an answer," Michelle said. Then, changing her mind as she pulled on Bill's arms until he was standing, she said, "Bite me."

"Tempting," he answered, "but I have a morbid fear of rabies."

Dean pulled her cell phone out of her pack and called her

mother. Michelle asked her to come pick them up. "Let's get you across the street where it's not blocked off. Think you can make it, old thing?"

"Yeah, Mick, you do prefer young meat. How old would you say Metterschmidt is? In his late-twenties? Aren't you a bit long in the tooth for him?"

"Since when did thirty-three become fossil fodder?"

"Since when were you thirty-three? At your birthday bash last month there was an inferno of no fewer than thirty-five candles."

In just a few minutes, Michelle spotted her mother and waved her down. "Thirty-three, thirty-five, who cares?" she challenged.

"Evidently you do."

"Are you two still bickering? Don't you ever stop?" Janice Dean asked, getting out of the car to check on Haldeman's wounds.

Michelle opened the trunk and pulled out a stadium blanket, spreading it over the back seat. "Put Mr. Clumsy back here," she instructed her mother. "Don't wanna get contaminated body fluids all over your car."

As Janice gently helped Haldeman into the vehicle, she asked her daughter, "Do you think he needs some stitches? Is his nose broken? Should I take him to a hospital?"

A nasal twang emanated from the back seat. "HE will be okay as soon as HE takes a warm shower and tapes up HIS nose."

"Did you hear something, Mother?" Michelle said as the two women climbed into the car, their long legs making the task tricky.

When they got to the Dean's, they unfolded themselves, helped Haldeman into the house, and left him in the bathroom while they headed into the kitchen to down some coffee. "I haven't asked about your specific duty while you're here," Janice said, her blue eyes looking into her daughter's green ones. "I know sometimes you can't tell me, but I always worry if it's too dangerous."

"What do you define as too dangerous?" Michelle asked, snaking her hand through the wet, blonde hair she'd released from her soaking sweatband.

"Let's see," her mother said. "Getting shot would be first; shooting someone else would rank second, and any other injury that would blot out one of your six senses or disassemble any important body parts."

"Mom, we've had this discussion before. It says in the job description that I might get a boo-boo now and then," she smiled over the rim of her mug. "But this time, I'm not the one you should be worrying about; it's the gubernatorial candidates who seem to be taking the heat."

Janice placed some chocolate cookies on a plate between them. "I know. Isn't it awful? Why would anyone want to harm a Democrat? The Republicans I can understand. But who would want to kill that nice Professor Vance?"

"A guy named Rick who's still in the hospital, still comatose, so he can't tell us why." Michelle devoured her second cookie. Her mother continued to look at her with a pained expression. "I didn't shoot him, Mom."

"Well, I'm sure this Rick person is a Republican."

Michelle shrugged. Her mother had been a staunch Democrat since Harry Truman fired Douglas MacArthur and Camelot gasped its last along with the two kings, JFK and Martin Luther. All Republicans, Janice averred, had eyes that were set too close together plus they were big old liarheads. Janice was the daughter of an 80 acre farmer and the wife of a small businessman who never made it. She presided over the local Democratic machine and was also a radical left-winger, as well as a junior high English teacher.

"Mom, tell me what's bad about the candidates that are left. What's your take on the whole thing?"

"You really want to know?"

"Yeah, what issues are explosive as far as you're concerned?

Are any of them so controversial that the men and women who are touting them should be killed?"

Her mother poured them both some more coffee and turned the air conditioning down. Janice greeted Haldeman, fresh from a shower and, Michelle thought, looking less like a crash dummy and more like a child who had taken a tumble. "How about a cup of coffee?" she asked.

He shook his head. "Don't you two know it's a hundred and ten degrees in the shade today?"

Janice chuckled. "I just can't give up my coffee. But I turned the air conditioner down to 68, are you uncomfortable?"

Haldeman pushed a glass under the ice machine slot and filled it with the water from the same outlet in the refrigerator door. "Water will be fine with me. Think I lost most of my fluids trying to make it up those . . . er . . . darn hills you have around here."

"Darn?" Michelle queried. "Since when did your word choice become so PC?"

Glaring at her, he turned to Janice and shook his head. "Your daughter has the mistaken idea that I am uncivilized and uncouth. I assure you that nobody is more couth than me."

"Than *I*," Janice corrected. She blushed. "Oh, I'm sorry. I've been a teacher too long."

Michelle snorted as her mother pulled out a chair for the dark-haired, solidly built man. "I was just asking Mom to go over any gripes she might have about the political platforms for us. Maybe it's not the people but the program."

"Sounds good," Haldeman agreed. "I've been so involved in background issues and gathering personal information that I haven't really studied the issues."

Michelle knew there was nothing closer to her mother's heart than politics. Unfortunately they'd only hear one side, and hear it in detail at a decibel level that had been known to crack fresh hen's eggs.

"The very worst thing is that some want to abolish the Department of Education and the Environmental Protection Agency. Now what's that all about?" Janice said. "How could they?" She picked up her coffee mug and spilled its contents on her beachcombers. "Damn."

"I think they should all be killed." Michelle winked at Haldeman. "How about hog lots?" she whispered, trying to give her mother a hint about her vocal range.

"Hog lots?" Her mother looked blank.

"Yeah, Mom, Louella Strong, the Republican Lieutenant Governor candidate, says she is opposed to turning piggies over to conglomerates that push the small farmer out of business."

"Oh," Janice blinked. "Yes, I read that. You know, I'll bet that woman is more Democrat than Republican. I'd root for her in a second if she'd just switch to the right party. I wonder if her parents deluded her?"

Michelle could no longer keep herself together after that comment. She stood up, laughing so hard that tears flooded down her cheeks and she could only gasp, "Parents try to influence their offspring? Naw. No way."

"All right, Miss Smarty Pants, that's enough." Janice took the cookies away from her daughter and shoved them toward Bill. "Just see if I don't beat you in the race. Then we'll see who's a good influence. I've been letting you win for the last five years, but no more Ms. Nice Guy from now on."

Michelle bent to give her mother a hug and a kiss. "I never believed you weren't the best." Turning to Bill she asked, "Well, since I only have three days until she stomps me into dust, how do you want to handle checking out the sites where the candidates will be?" ✤

✤ In the few days before the hordes began to flood into the Mississippi river town, the agents learned that the man who called himself Father Metterschmidt planned a rally on the main stage in the center of downtown, and that Van Der Boomsma was going to be holding court at the new, plush Radisson while Louella had decided on the personal approach, milling through the crowds and shaking hands. The Democrats were being covered by two other agents assigned by Governor Vilsack.

"You suppose Kim and Mel are better agents than we are, agent 11 and 3/4?" Dean asked Haldeman while they watched the vendors setting up shops along three blocks of Second Street.

"Naw, but they're better Democrats. I'm a registered Independent. And I don't think Vilsack's met your mother."

As they stood there, Metterschmidt strolled by with a chubby, short woman and a child. He stopped in front of the workers who were erecting the stage for the local bands and his speech tomorrow. "What do you think, Mel?" he queried.

"Are they going to have risers for our choir?" the woman asked.

The handsome Father frowned down at her from his six foot two, muscled frame. "Melissa, my dear, the only person who should stand higher than me is God." He threw back his head and laughed heartily. She fingered the gold lavaliere that hung on the chain around her neck. It looked like either a fraternity symbol or a fat-topped cross.

Haldeman made an unappetizing noise and the priest turned. "Ah, sorry," Bill said, "my sinuses." He pointed to his nose.

"Looks like yours were attacked," Father Metterschmidt said.

Michelle bubbled a laugh. "No, he had a fight with some asphalt and the asphalt won."

Metterschmidt peered more closely at her. "Don't I know you?"

"Ah . . . well . . . yeah, we met at the mall the other day. In front of the ice cream store?"

He snapped his fingers. "Oh, yes. Well, I hope you got your ice cream home all right."

The little girl tugged on the priest's shirttail. "Phillip," she whined, "you said you'd buy me some ice cream. When you gonna? Huh?"

"Shortly, Amy." He smiled at Michelle. "Oh, where are my manners? This is Melissa Anchor and her daughter, Amy." He held out his arm to Haldeman and, as the two shook hands, he said, "Doctor Phil." Then he turned back to Melissa and said, "Mel this is . . . ah . . ."

"Michelle. Michelle Dean. And this is my . . . er . . . friend, Billy Haldeman." She gripped her partner's shoulder, squeezing to make sure he didn't give them away. It was obvious the doctor or priest still didn't have the foggiest idea they were special agents. It occurred to her that they had been introduced in uniform when they were assigned to watch over this man, but then, anyone this pretty didn't have to possess a perfect memory.

The women nodded to each other. Michelle turned to gaze at the tall, Brad Pitt re-creation and asked, "Ah . . . what kind of a doctor are you, medical or educated?" His eyes crinkled as she amended, "Not that medical doctors aren't educated. What I meant to say . . ."

Doctor Phil let her off the hook. "I know, pretty lady, and to answer you, I have my Ph.D. in Religion."

There were three dimples on his face, one on his chin and deeper ones in each cheek. Now how cute was that? So, was he a priest too? She didn't dare ask him, since he was not wearing the collar either time she saw him in Davenport.

The well-padded blonde woman shushed her child who was still grabbing Phil's shirttail and repeating, "Ice cream, now. Ice cream now."

Metterschmidt said to Haldeman and Dean, "I'm going to be speaking here tomorrow at 4:00. I hope you can make it."

Michelle gazed into eyes the color of gray you can see through right down into the soul. His high cheekbones, pouty lips, and longish blond hair all combined to make her knees weak. She might have trouble keeping up with him in the Bix race with melty knees and all.

Haldeman grabbed her elbow as Melissa Anchor and her daughter came back. "C'mon" he said, "we have work to do." Then he dragged Michelle away. The father's group walked over to the workmen.

"What the devil?" Michelle asked, pulling her arm away.

Haldeman hissed, "Melissa Anchor. The DCI interviewed her, remember? After Vance's killing? She was a campaign worker for Vance. I was there. I guess I made as much impression on her as you did on Phil baby."

"So what's she doing with Doctor M.?"

"Ya got me. Maybe she fell under his spell like someone else who's name I won't mention who just happens to be standing next to me panting like Claridge's boxer, Winston."

Marching away from him, Michelle hurled back, "Jealous?"

Bill didn't answer. ✤

✤ The next day the partners were down at the bottom of Brady Street with 20,000 others. They had arrived early and Haldeman had positioned himself near Louella Strong. Michelle was just a bit behind Father Metterschmidt. The priest and she had to wait a good three minutes before their line was even able to start up the vertical street. She imagined it would be five or more for Strong and Haldeman.

The awesome sight of the runners clogging the street, legs pumping, heads bobbing, never ceased to thrill Michelle. She kept up with the handsome man, even though seeing him in runner's shorts and a tee shirt was not helping her race breathing. His muscles rippled and undulated as he effortlessly trotted in front of her. The Bix was a friendly race, if you weren't one of the front runners, and the good father slapped a lot of hands belonging to the bystanders that clapped and yelled encouragement along the race route. Most of those hands, Michelle noticed, were attached to arms that led up to necks circled by the same necklace worn by Melissa Anchor and Amy.

As Michelle and Father Metterschmidt made their way down Kirkwood, she saw Bill and Louella coming up on the other side of the boulevard that separated the course. She waved, but he didn't see her. Louella was keeping a good pace, strong and sure, and poor Bill looked a bit like a lobster before it gets thrown in the pot. It wasn't because he was in poor shape, Michelle knew; it was that the heat really bothered him. He'd grown up on the upper peninsula of Michigan where it never became really hot hot. When he joined the service just three years ago, she'd asked him why he came to Iowa since he complained loud and long about the summer weather. "I came here because there was a job here, and I stayed because there was a you here." It was one of the few times he'd showed any feelings for her. Of course, she'd been practically engaged to a guy, and then had broken up with him—about the same time as Bill started going out with a buxom state trooper.

Michelle hit the top of Brady and almost fell forward. It was always a surprise when she learned, all over again, that going downhill at this steep a pitch was harder than going up. Her calves were not happy with this new torture, but she finally shot into the women's chute, glancing briefly at the timer. She'd done very well. Better than last year, at least. She cooled down walking through the festival of food set up especially for the runners. The place was packed; she didn't see her mother. But she was really looking for the pretty Doc Phil.

Sitting on the grass, cross-legged, her eyes scanning the crowd, she dug into a strawberry yogurt. Bill plopped down beside her, panting, his arms full of free goodies. He was sopping wet.

"Run through every water station on the route?"

He shook his head, obviously unable to speak, but pointed to a booth across from them. Louella was smiling, looking cool and together, introducing herself, asking for support as her aides passed out bumper stickers and buttons and water bottles decorated with her name and the slogan, "Vote for a STRONG Iowa." Slick idea.

As soon as Bill could breathe almost normally, the two agents headed for their car, after checking with the local police to make sure their charges were in good hands, and drove to Janice's house for showers and a change. When they returned to the streets of downtown, the street fest was in full swing. Smells of charcoal, butterfly pork chops, roasted almonds, beer, and sweat filled the humid air, making it almost chewable. The noise of the revelers made it impossible to confer with each other, so Michelle dragged Haldeman down a block to the Radisson, which not only held Van Der Boomsma, but cops with walkie talkies that could tell them where Ph.D. Metterschmidt and Louella were now.

The Republican candidate for governor was imitating his name by booming out catch phrases like "big business" and "prosperity." The same old party line. Michelle wondered briefly if her mother's influence hadn't been overkill in her case. Red, white and blue bunting hung from the atrium, reflecting the colors that festooned *The Rhythm City* riverboat. Louella was now on the bow of the floating casino, talking with a crowd.

Metterschmidt evidently had been taken to a house in Bettendorf, Davenport's sister city and a place its mayor called Camelot, Iowa's Most Exciting City. It was a bedroom community full of doctors, lawyers, company executives, and fine schools, but the only thing exciting about it, before the *Lady Luck Casino* landed, was a hardware store. Of course, the gambling boat was afloat in the Mississippi River, and the rich people lived up the hill in their enormous piles of brick and stucco.

Haldeman made his way to Louella, and Dean drove to the address she'd been given. There was a squad car in front of the house on Saint Andrew Circle which backed up to the exclusive Crow Creek Golf Course and Club. She parked down the street and strolled up, stopping to talk with the cop, casually, raising no suspicion. The cop introduced himself and handed her a sophisticated squawk box which would allow him to inform her of Metterschmidt and his movements. Michelle thanked him and went back to downtown Davenport looking for Van Der Boomsma. She found him surrounded by what looked like bought and paid for bodyguards along with half the Davenport police force. She wandered around, eating a huge plate of home-fried potato chips, a brat with everything, and downing three fresh lemonades. Then she made her way to the levee where she found a square of cool grass shaded by a maple tree.

Plopping down, she leaned against the tree and enjoyed the brassy sounds of the Dixieland group in the band shell. She blinked out of a dream when her beeper sounded and the Bettendorf police force squawk box erupted. Metterschmidt, the cop told her, had left the house about half an hour ago and then had given him the slip. Bill also was beeping. She glanced at her watch and discovered it was close to 4:00. Using her cell phone, she dialed Bill's.

"What's up?" she asked. She couldn't hear him above the noise at his end. "Where are you?"

He shouted something that sounded like Second Street and Brady, then repeated it. Michelle grabbed her backpack and ran the three blocks to the corner. She had trouble muscling her way toward the center of the mob. But, when she got there, all she could see was a cordon of Davenport's finest, guns drawn, surrounding what must be an accident. Bill cut through the center of the group when he spotted her. A yapping dog followed his heels until he was on the other side of the cop circle. There was no doubt the canine was Winston. So, was the body . . .?"

Bill took her hand. "It's Claridge. He's been shot. Not fatally, I don't think."

"Why?" Michelle looked into her partner's eyes. "What kind of a threat was he?"

"I've been thinking about that," he whispered into her ear, his hot breath tickling her neck. "He was the only possible candidate the Democrats had, considering the nonmainstream habits of the rest. Now there's no one."

A woman elbowed her way to beside them. It was Louella Strong. Her mouth opened and then clamped shut, a faint smile twitching the edges. Across from them, Michelle spotted Catherine Shark. The Democrat's face was hard to read, but no tears fell.

From the stage behind them came a booming announcement, garbled because of the crowd voices, but words filtered into Michelle's brain. "Candidate . . . Reform Party . . . Phil . . . Doctor . . . Metterschmidt." Then it sounded as if a good old Iowa thunderstorm was crackling and rumbling through the listeners. And, as suddenly as the roar went up, it came down. A choir, whether from heaven or the stage behind them, began to sing sweetly, "Shall We Gather at the River." The people around the body quieted also as they listened to the music and watched the paramedics lift the still bleeding Winston Claridge onto a gurney. A fitting song.

As this crowd thinned, Dean and Haldeman followed the wave of humanity toward the stage behind them. The agents stood to the side so they could see both the speaker and the crowd. A man ran out from behind the stage and looked toward the choir. Michelle spotted Melissa Anchor, front row center in the choir, who gave him an exaggerated shrug. He, in turn, gave a signal to the choir director to keep it rolling. The choir launched into "Nearer My God to Thee," which Michelle knew had been played by the musicians on the *Titanic*. She knotted her brow. Another fitting song?

Haldeman, who had moved away, came back and poked her side, pointing out Louella Strong and Catherine Sharp deep in conversation. Michelle raised her right eyebrow. Smiling broadly, he reported he'd overheard Louella say, "Van Der Boomsma and I aren't the closest of running mates, but he's got the party's deep pockets and the truth is, I'll be more effective in the statehouse than walking the corn . . . ." Bill also heard Catherine remark so softly that he practically fell on the two, "Well, I don't know what will happen now that the clown has been shot . . . . I don't agree with the song that there have to be clowns, but I'm glad we're not sending in this one . . . . Of course, I don't wish him dead, just out of the race . . . ."

"Holy Hannah," Michelle said, "did they say anything about Doctor Phil?"

Haldeman shook his head. He opened his mouth but before he could say anything more, the behind-the-stage-man came out and yelled into the microphone, "And now, the Reform Party's Man of the Hour, Doctor Phillip Metterschmidt."

Father Metterschmidt spun onto the stage, smiling a 200 watter, and launched into a speech. "Loyal followers, pretty ladies and handsome men, Iowa's finest citizens, I beckon you to a new age of truth and prosperity under the Reform Party banner." The audience was mesmerized; his charismatic presence seeming to fill the outdoors.

Bill hissed in her ear, "Well, so you aren't the only pretty woman here."

Michelle shushed him. The choir began humming "The Battle Hymn of the Republic" as Metterschmidt continued, "To the farmers of our great state I promise prosperity. To our fine golden-agers I offer support both financially and spiritually. To you businessmen I encourage your wishes that Iowa grow, and I beseech you to become an important part of a brand new Iowa under the Reform Party platform. To all you who believe, who know of the new era about to burst forth, accept me as your leader. Let us move forward as soldiers marching into battle . . . ." The choir's voices soared into "Onward Christian Soldiers," and the crowd was again on its feet, cheering, keeping a clapping beat with the strident hymn.

Michelle felt dizzy, whether from the magnetism of this man or the gold crosses on gold chains that swung in rhythm to the song both in the choir and in the audience. She stumbled backwards. Bill caught her, wrapping his arms securely around her, sitting her down on his lap on the pavement.

"Mick, Mick, you all right?" he cried.

She twisted to look at her partner, her eyes threatening to overflow with emotion. "Isn't he . . . isn't he . . ."

"A nutcase?" Bill said.

Michelle shook her head which seemed to clear things up a bit. "No, you creep. Isn't he . . . gorgeous?"

Bill didn't answer.

STEPHANIE KEENAN, *ex-English teacher and current freelance writer, book doctor, and president of the Stephawk Agency, lives in Bettendorf, Iowa. She has written a weekly humor column for the* Bettendorf News *as well as essays on the plight of the writing teacher in today's schools. Stephawk strives to place author clients into seminars or conferences where they teach everything from beginning novel-writing to screenwriting. Stephanie has recently completed two private eye novels and a screenplay about randy angels angry at the Creator, who turns out to be a wiry, ancient old lady who has a New Jersey accent. The Creator is threatening to destroy humankind if the womanly angels can't wrest the power back from men. Stephanie believes in angels, Tom Robbins, P. G. Wodehouse, and laughter.*

12.

Walkin' the Dog

By Carole Shelley Yates

By the time Iowa's corn-growing season arrived in early August, the Democrats were still committed to sending in their clown, as some called nominee Winston Claridge. The gunshot hit him in the left arm, a near miss to the heart. But far enough away that Claridge was still in the race, and, with the help of consultants, was actually pulling together a serious campaign.

Knowing their candidate was alive and kicking, his aides and volunteers rallied for a heavy-duty strategy meeting now that the election was only three months away. Offering the workers breakfast goodies induced them to attend the early morning meeting at Claridge's Cedar Rapids home where he was quickly recovering.

"O.K., here's the deal," Claridge said to the small group gathered in the sunroom. "We're going to focus on that damned Republican Ed Van Der Boomsma. I just don't think the Reform Party candidate Metterschmidt has a chance in spit of getting far in this campaign. He's starting way too late, that priest, or doctor, or whatever he is today."

"Excuse me sir," interrupted one of his aides, "but a lot of religious people do have doctoral degrees. It's not unusual. It just means he might be someone to contend with if he's so knowledgeable."

"Oh hell," Claridge retorted. "The Reform Party's never been strong in Iowa. I think our main focus needs to be the Republicans. We're going to hire some more staffers. I've got the money for sure now. Getting shot was the best thing that could have happened to my campaign. I got a lot of press coverage. I've moved from last place before the primaries to first place. Hey, anything can happen, so let's play that sympathy vote for all it's worth.

"And while we're at it, let's see if we can dig up some dirt on Van Der Boomsma. Who are his Pella connections, his statewide connections? Why did he agree to step in suddenly to be the Republican fall guy? And who is going around shooting all the candidates anyway? The bumbling DCI isn't helping much— maybe we can find something on Van Der Boomsma that we can use closer to November. For now, we've got some topnotch consultants to help us put this thing together."

Among the supporters listening to the longest, most coherent speech in Claridge's political career was one major surprise: Candy Fairfield. The ambitious wife of former candidate Alan Fairfield and a woman known to stop at nothing for political gain, Candy saw the handwriting on the wall for her future. She used her "expertise" to convince Claridge to name her the lieutenant governor candidate on the Democratic ticket.

"Balls," she thought, "if Alan's not likely to be moving to Des Moines, I'll see what I can do about getting myself ensconced as close as possible to Terrace Hill. Iowa's had several female lieutenant governors, and with Claridge's track record at bumbling and getting shot, this could be a prime opportunity. Hey, I lived with Alan's sexual propensities; it hasn't been that tough to meet Claridge's needs. And it got me my place on the ticket."

Claridge introduced Candy as Iowa's next Lieutenant Governor and she gave her official political tight-lipped smile, designed to please all and get all she was after. Campaign excitement grew as Candy announced the "legwork" she'd been doing while Claridge was recovering from "arm work." In fact, she was determined to run the campaign, and run it her way, she thought, placing her silver-lacquered fingernails on her svelte hips as she prepared to speak.

"Because Winston's been laid up, he asked me to do some organizing. I've done this a million times for Alan's campaigns. I got lucky and met with Christy and Tom Vilsack who kindly agreed to help out the Democrats," Candy explained as the staffers awaited their next assignments.

"Here are their two big ideas that will get this campaign moving. Christy, with her background in journalism, suggested that Winston needs to balance his unDemocratic big business background with a pro-environmental strategy. And adding to that, Tom gave us the scoop on how his office handled the walking tour of Iowa in the spring and summer of 2000 to hear what Iowans had to say. So—with Winston's approval," she added, looking at Claridge as if they shared a dirty little secret, "that's the direction we're headed now. We've got to make plans to kick off the walking campaign at Backbone State Park where Winston will make a pro-environmental statement about the need to keep some natural areas in our corn and soybean-drenched state."

Candy, herself a staunch environmental supporter and member of the Iowa Natural Heritage Foundation and Sierra Club, punched her hand in the air to make her point, being careful not to drop the chocolate-covered doughnut she held. True to her name, Candy loved chocolate. As she let her arm fall, she felt a nudge at the wrist and the doughnut immediately disappeared into Winston, the dog's, drooling boxer lips.

Candy quickly stepped aside before the 75-pound overly friendly boxer could sit on her feet, demanding of Winston the candidate, "Where did you ever get this beast and why do you keep him?"

"Well," chuckled the ample candidate, "Ol' Winnie originally belonged to my sister, Sherry, and her family. But they begged me to take him since I'm on my own and they thought my household wouldn't offer as many temptations for the dog."

"What do you mean temptations?" Candy wanted to know, her lurid mind filling with bizarre and revolting sexual fantasies now that she had to spend time with the candidate and the dog.

"Oh, that dog, he's a smart one he is," explained Claridge. "Why, one day my sister left out the fixings for chocolate chip cookies on the counter. And while she was gone, Winnie got his front paws up on the counter and proceeded to eat the ingredients—butter, eggs (in the shell, naturally), and most of the 5-pound sack of flour as well. I never knew a dog could eat so much and not get sick. One Halloween he got into my nephew's room and ate his Halloween candy, wrappers, gum, and all, before Chris even had time to count his loot."

"Hmm, I'll remember to keep my things put away," Candy muttered, wondering if this campaign was going to be worth the work, the mental anguish, and the annoyance of putting up with Winston the dog's idiosyncratic eating habits. Still, she figured they couldn't be worse than Claridge's habits. She looked at him with his left arm in a sling, trying to lace his fingers across his substantial belly, and she knew he, too, had consumed his share of chocolate chip cookie ingredients. But, she quickly assured herself, she could put aside her own revulsion in the interest of her personal Terrace Hill promotional project.

The strategy meeting concluded with numerous assignments to pull together the kick-off event at Backbone State Park. One staffer was assigned to hire more workers, including a few with experience from former candidates' campaigns. Someone suggested Melissa Anchor, who'd worked for Dr. Vance's campaign before his untimely fall. Another staffer was asked to hire a rock-climbing group to demonstrate climbing techniques at the Backbone kick-off. ✤

✤ Fortunately for the Democratic gubernatorial candidate and his crew, the summer of 2002 in Iowa had been a dry one. Although that meant potential problems for the farm constituency, it also meant fewer mosquitoes across the state. And if you planned to kick off an event at Backbone State Park, the fewer mosquitoes the better.

But any event outdoors in a park caused DCI Special Agents Dean and Haldeman to feel major headaches coming on. It was a literal pain when candidates had to be covered in such vulnerable situations.

Along with the rest of the Claridge entourage (the Republicans may have called it a cortege), Dean and Haldeman found themselves winding their way along Delaware County Highway C64 outside of Dundee toward the east entrance to Backbone State Park. Since Claridge had ben shot, Dean and Haldeman had been added to his contingent of guards. Dean, sitting in the passenger's front seat, watched the goldenrod and black-eyed susans flash by in the ditches. Soon the line of cars wound its way through Backbone, past the castle tower bathhouse on the lake where the hot August day provided perfect weather for pastel-colored paddle boats and their paddlers to be out on the lake.

"I sure wish we hadn't drawn the job of covering this kick-off," groused Dean. She loved the outdoors and would rather have been part of the rock climbing group Claridge had hired to show the wonders of the state park instead of working on a clear summer day. Or, she thought, her perfect assignment would be covering Father/Dr. Phil who was holding his own press event at Backbone's CCC Museum at the north end of the park. Strange, though, that Father Metterschmidt chose to hold his event in the same state park on the same day as the Democrats.

Haldeman interrupted her reverie. "At least we get to stand outside," he noted, "and I hope we don't have to rescue any candidates today. I've had enough of this knock 'em off one-by-one stuff.

What did you hear from our profiler about possible suspects?"

Dean shifted her position in the front seat of the Ford Taurus run on Iowa ethanol, and explained the latest before they got to the 50 foot limestone bluff where the Claridge event was scheduled to begin at 2 p.m.

"First of all, I'm sad to say, no one seems to be able to track down what institution Dr. Phil got his degree from. So is he a priest, a university professor, or a mystery for the *Catholic Messenger* to unravel from its correct or mislabeled file photos?

"But more to the point, the DCI profiler thinks the motive for all of the killings is so complex that more than one person is involved. So now we're on the lookout for who knows how many suspects? This thing gets crazier by the minute."

Haldeman steered the car around the winding road, past the limestone sign etched with "Backbone State Park" that marked the beginning of the famous trail that looked and felt like you were walking on a prehistoric creature's backbone.

"The reporter for the *Register*, Drew Wright, called me last night to say he's continued with his original investigation of Bob Blackwell's unsavory, illegitimate dealings and thinks he's come onto a possible connection with Van Der Boomsma," Haldeman said, adding another suspect. "They've gotten money from the same special interest groups—the NRA, tobacco companies . . . . In fact, Wright hears rumblings that Farmer Van Der Boomsma's grain elevators may have been used to store something other than grain . . . something like mislabeled soybeans headed to Japan."

"Where did he hear that?" Dean yelled, but her question was drowned out by a voice over a loudspeaker announcing the beginning of Winston Claridge's press event. The agents were all business as they parked, got out of the car, and hurried to their assigned area beside a flatbed truck which served as a makeshift stage at the base of the cliff. ✤

✤ Insinuating herself into situations was one of Melissa Anchor's better honed skills. She'd been assigned to the Vance campaign to deliver information and found it just as easy to join Winston Claridge's staff. After all, she had some experience, so she was quickly hired based on Claridge's philosophy "if it worked for someone else, I'll try it too—Vance's aide, Strong's plasma pumping, Vilsack's cross-Iowa jaunt—whatever."

The set-up was a win-win (maybe) situation: Claridge hired Melissa as an events coordinator and Melissa would learn more about the Democrat's campaign plans. The only drawback for Melissa was Candy Fairfield horning into the lieutenant governor's candidacy. Melissa had thought Candy was a shrewd self-promoter when she first met her, and now she felt Candy would do anything to promote her own personal interests.

"Her name might be Candy, but she's no treat to work with. This assignment may not be as easy as the Vance one," Melissa thought as she stood by the makeshift stage she'd helped set up near the jagged climbing bluff. Claridge now seemed absorbed with the money his computer business was making and content to leave the bulk of the campaign planning to that tight-lipped Candy Fairfield.

On the other hand, Melissa Anchor herself had done some growing up since she worked for Dr. Vance's campaign in the spring. She was no longer just the "chubby chick" as some reporter had called her after seeing her picture in the paper with former, now dead, candidate Bob Blackwell.

"Dead," she murmured. "That wasn't supposed to be part of the deal. I said I'd help expose Bob Blackwell as a louse. But murder? Whoa, this whole thing is going too far, too fast."

During the spring and early summer, as one candidate after another "disappeared," Melissa had done her own thinking. She wasn't so sure the "mission" was her mission any longer. In fact, she was getting tired of putting up with a suffocating situation where she was told in detail what to do with her life and who to be.

But today at Backbone, Melissa's mission was to get the show on the road with this kick-off event. She'd come a long way from her flower-arranging days with Dr. Vance in the spring to having some real responsibility with a campaign in August. She was ready to get down to business, especially with her mind at ease now that her four-year-old daughter Amy was staying with Vance's sister, who Melissa met during the primary campaign. Melissa was reassured because Peg Vance had teenage children who were watching Amy while Peg, another Dr. Vance, spent her time studying the dreams of fruit flies in the entomology department at the University of Iowa.

"Today is a big day for me," Melissa mused as she watched the candidate and his aides pour out of their cars and make their way to the stage, skirted with red, white, and blue bunting.

"Ohhhh," she groaned, getting dizzy as she looked up, "not only do I have to see that this kick-off goes off without a hitch, but old Winston also wants me to be the guinea pig to do some amateur rock climbing so he can prove that he's for the environment and natural spaces. He's got his bum arm so he can't do it and that irritating, pushy Candy won't. Even when I told him I was afraid of heights he wouldn't listen, so I'm the chosen one for the publicity stunt." ❖

❖ As the political press and security crews gathered at the designated spot, Agents Dean and Haldeman spotted Drew Wright from the *Register* and made their way across the mowed grassy area to buttonhole him about the Van Der Boomsma information. But Wright was in no mood for serious stuff.

"I can't wait for the climbing to begin," he enthused to the agents, not responding to their questions. "I haven't climbed since my Boy Scout days when we were at this very bluff. I'll never forget when our senior patrol leader—that's SPL—climbed up the bluff and tried to rappel down. See that basswood tree growing right out of the cliff? That goofy SPL kicked out from the wall too far and landed smack in the top of that very tree—he looked like a big bird plopped on a nest!"

Wright watched as the climbers below took out the gear from their bags—the special climbing ropes of braided nylon, the seat harnesses, the carabiners. Above, he could barely see other climbers at the top of the jagged bluff tying lark's head knots to fashion anchor ropes. It looked like it would be a real challenge to climb this wall the way the climbing group had it set up for a demonstration. The climbers were outfitting the high bluff with two ropes, one to climb up and one to rappel down. That meant at the top the climbers would have to unclip their rope from the climbing carabiner on their harness and then clip themselves onto the rappelling rope. But to change ropes, the climbers would have to scale the lip overhang to reach the top of the cliff thick with brush.

Wright watched the operation, wanting to do the climb himself. "Yeh, climbing is a real rush, but it's also a dangerous sport," he lectured the special agents. "You have to have complete trust in the people who set up the climbing and rappelling anchor ropes at the top of the bluff. If you don't have the ropes anchored to a strong enough tree or rock, well . . . your life really is in their hands . . . ."

Reluctantly, Wright turned his attention to Winston Claridge and to Candy Fairfield, the Democrat's newly named running mate. Standing side by side, they kicked off their campaign as they announced their walking tour of Iowa—"Walkin' the Dog," in honor of Claridge's dear boxer.

As if upon command, Winston the dog pushed his way between Claridge and Fairfield. Jowls quivering, he jumped up to land a big slobbery slurp on Candy's face. "My god," she blurted, losing all poise and roughly shoving the dog backward. "Why, oh why, did I have to have an edible name?" She haltingly patted her auburn-tinted hair back into its careful arrangement.

The crowd loved it. It took awhile for them to quiet down to hear the candidates explain their environmental platform and why parts of Iowa should remain natural.

"Some people want Backbone to become a Destination Park for our state," Claridge awkwardly read from a script Fairfield had written. "That's a thought, but not a good one. We shouldn't ruin what we have here. It's a natural area and there aren't many left in the state. A Destination Park with bike trails, cabins, swimming pool, horseback riding, and a nice lake for boating would be great for Iowa. But let's start from scratch, not ruin something as pristine as Backbone State Park. We need places like Backbone," he intoned, "and places like a Destination Park if we're ever going to keep young people in our state or attract new workers to Iowa. I propose that we keep natural areas and develop new parks that invite people to participate in the prairie atmosphere our state came from.

"Now one of the special things about Backbone is its remarkable limestone bluffs. Our state is built mostly on limestone bedrock, and at Backbone one way to appreciate it is by climbing it. We've invited a local climbing group to help us out today as they show one of my staff members just how easy it is to appreciate nature in the air."

While Claridge gave his spiel, Melissa was following the climbing instructor's directions as she stepped into her seat harness, strapped on her red helmet, laced up some borrowed climbing shoes, and tried not to think about her fear of heights. Swallows swooped down and around the bluffs, darting into holes in the cliffs as Melissa's fingers dug into her palms. She tried to remember to breathe.

She stepped in front of the bluff which up close looked impossible to climb. Where do you put your feet and hands? she wondered. But that's why Claridge had hired the climbing group, to tell her exactly what to do. Her chubby thighs lopped over the tight harness as the instructor—the one to belay her up the cliff—attached the rope with a figure eight knot to the "beener" clipped to the center of her harness, and finally back through his harness so he became her anchor on the ground. He then gave her the climbing commands.

"The first thing you say is 'up rope,' which means I'll tighten the rope on your harness. You'll always be on the rope and I can help pull you up, so not to worry. You can even kick back from the cliff and swing in mid-air and be safe. So, if your hands get tired, say 'take,' to warn me you want to let go of the rope and rest a bit."

"Ya sure, and I'm Peter Pan," Melissa mocked with a quaver in her voice.

But the instructor seemed competent. All she could do was trust his skill, certainly not her own. They went through the rest of the climbing commands.

"Finally, if you don't think you can make it all the way to the top and you want to come down, say 'dirt me' and I'll lower you," concluded the instructor.

"Dirt me, right," Melissa said, sure she'd land in the dirt head first instead of on her feet.

The Claridge aide, her blonde hair getting sticky on the back of her neck, began to climb, putting each hand and foot exactly where the instructor designated.

"Use your legs . . ." the instructor urged her. "Pull up a little with your hands and then push up with your legs."

Melissa tried her best to use her stumpy legs and not look down. "Just look straight ahead," she told herself. "Look at the crack in the limestone; study that fern growing out of a crevice; look at the spots of dew on each leaf . . . ."

Gradually she made progress, while on the ground the political hotshots paid her little attention. Instead they were focused on Claridge and Fairfield as they explained the goals of the "Walkin' the Dog" tour to small Iowa towns.

"We'll start in Strawberry Point at the S.P. Food Mart," explained Candy Fairfield, recovering her aplomb after Winston's indignities, taking charge in her best organizational tone. "Then we'll move on to other parts of northeast Iowa . . . Postville, Fayette, Decorah . . . and then into other sections of our state so we hear from people in many parts of Iowa. And yes, we'll be walking Winston, the delightful doggie, most of the way. It's a good thing Candidate Claridge was shot in the arm and not the leg," she laughed. "He can still walk his dog to meet and hear from as many Iowans as possible."

On the cliff, Melissa Anchor wished she'd never agreed to continue with the "mission." She must have been crazy to do it for all sorts of reasons, number one being her fear of heights, and number two her fear of death—hers and others.

"I thought I believed in our mission," she considered as she reached for the next handhold on the perpendicular cliff. "But, I don't know. I just don't know any more. Maybe what we're doing isn't right."

She was getting closer to the top of the bluff where one of the climbing group was supposed to pull her past the overhang and then help her unclip the climbing rope from the carabiner on her harness and clip it to the rappelling rope so she could get back down to the safe, solid ground.

She was almost at the cliff overhang, only slightly scraped from the sharp rocks. As she swung freely in mid-air from the climbing rope, she studied the cliff side, looking for hand or footholds to pull herself up and over the jut-out. She searched frantically, then yelled, "Help, I need help. I can't make it these last few inches to the top."

A man's large hands reached down toward her. The strong

hands pulled her past the overhang and into the brush on the top of the cliff on firm ground. Melissa let out a deep sigh of relief. Instantly, a scraggly beard appeared smack in her face, and the hands wrapped the climbing rope around her neck.

"There's a nasty rumor you're not happy with our mission anymore," the rough voice hissed at her. "You, you will do as you're instructed, or your daughter will be in real danger."

"Amy, Amy where is she?" Melissa said, grabbing the man's hairy arm.

"We know you've got her with that bug babe in Iowa City. So listen up now. If you keep saying things like you're losing your faith, Amy's gonna run into some serious problems, or some serious problems are gonna run into her," he said, breathing in Melissa's face. "That Fairfield broad is becoming a problem. Your mission now is to set up that clown Claridge's lieutenant clown so we can get at her, and you'll do it when we say," sneered the stranger.

Melissa, having forgotten all about her fear of heights, was trying to breathe as the rope tightened around her neck. The rope, the rope, she thought. She looked up; the sun hit her smack in the eyes and glinted off the chain around the stranger's neck.

With that threat, the grip around her neck loosened, and the stranger disappeared into the tall maple and oak trees. Melissa thought she heard the belayer on the ground ask if she'd given the "off rope" command. Visibly shaken, Melissa hoisted up her roundish figure, unaware of the cheers below. Belatedly, the audience noticed she'd made it to the top. She was scared, angry, and badly shaken. No way would she rappel down the cliff.

Where was the climber who was supposed to be at the top of the bluff to help her clip onto the rappelling rope?

"Hey," came a perturbed voice from below on the path. A young man wearing climbing pants and shoes approached her. "That guy with the beard was wrong. Nobody needed help at the bottom of the bluff like he told me. Gee, lady, you don't look too good. Are you o.k?" he quizzed her.

"No, I'm not o.k. I'm not o.k.," Melissa stuttered. "I've gotta get down the trail as fast as I can. My daughter . . . my daughter."

Unclipping the carabiner from the rope that had just threatened her life, Melissa bolted down the trail. When she reached the bottom, she grabbed a cell phone from one of the other aides and called the Vances in Iowa City. No answer. Starting to panic, Melissa realized she was calling attention to herself, the last thing she needed right now. She had to control herself for Amy's sake.

"All right," Melissa told herself trying to calm her inner chaos. "Get the job done, do what you're told, and find out about Amy. I can't let her get hurt . . . I can't. These true believers are downright dangerous . . . . They'll stop at nothing, and Amy is a whole lot more than nothing to me. My baby's everything!"

CAROLE SHELLEY YATES—*what a poetic name—writes and edits almost anything from her home office in Cedar Falls. As she concentrates on articles, newsletters, grants, and other publications, she can look out her east window at the white clouds of serviceberry shrubs, talk to the house finches at the window feeder, and hail the big bluestem grasses on the Iowa prairie she and her family are creating around their house. You may have read her work in* The Iowan, Iowa Commerce, *or* UNI's Northern Iowa Today *magazine. Or you may have heard her KUNI public radio commentaries or radio features on that station's award winning* Iowa's Remarkable Young Musicians *series.*

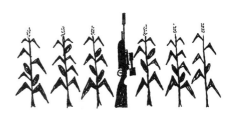

13.

Giving It the Old College Try

By Charles L. P. Silet

The handsome young male wearing sunglasses and dressed casually in a windbreaker and chinos stood looking across the central campus of Iowa State University. Students bustled along the sidewalks, backpacks slung over their shoulders. Some walked alone; others talked in pairs or jostled each other in groups. A mother strolled along holding the hand of a small boy.

Poor little tyke, he thought. He doesn't know yet that some day she'll dump him onto the world with no one to wipe his nose or give a rat's ass about him.

The man didn't often let himself think about his own mother. One day in the early 1970s while his father was still in Vietnam she just packed the boy's clothes in an old brown suitcase and dropped him off at his grandmother's; he never saw her again. Not even a phone call or letter over all of these years. But that was okay with him. Better to learn early than late that women couldn't be trusted.

When his father returned from the war, he showed up at the grandmother's house, repacked the brown suitcase, and hauled the toddler off to live in a cramped wreck of a trailer where he stayed until his father died, and every day of that time he was afraid and bewildered by his old man's strange behavior.

In between bouts of drug-induced paranoia and alcohol-fueled rages against the government, the Army, non-whites, women in general and the boy's mother in particular, his father beat into him everything the military had imparted about killing another human being. Never having been much of a success in the Army, his old man went in and came out a Private. But he did have one skill; he was extraordinarily adept at killing people, especially with a rifle, and the Army used this skill by making him a sniper. He would sit alone in the treetops and blow away the Viet Cong at three hundred yards. He was the best.

The boy grew up striving to please his father, and so learned his death skills well. He became a crack shot. First, plugging empty cans in the vacant lot behind the mobile home park and later, by himself in the woods, shooting birds, squirrels, anything that moved, he honed his technique. He would bring home these trophies hoping they would quiet his old man's rage and lift him out of his crushing depression. Later, of course, as an adult, he thought about all of this and made some sense of their lives and the lessons he was taught, but at the time the boy just cowered in his bed in the dark of the trailer, nursing his blinding headaches and praying to escape his daddy's wrath. ✜

✜ The man watched a Frisbee arch gracefully into the cloudless autumn sky and be snatched effortlessly by a young coed. She skimmed it on to a fellow student with a fluid flick of her wrist. Her friends yelled their approval and applauded her skill. The man frowned at their easy camaraderie, and her smug confidence.

What a mindless waste of time, he mused. What are these jerks here for, anyway?

The man remembered going off to school afraid and hungry, wearing his ill-fitting Salvation Army hand-me-downs. The kids taunted him unmercifully. He was always the last to be picked for games on the playground. The boys would beat him up on his way back to the trailer park, and the girls made fun of his clothes and his slowness in class.

But his dad taught him well, and he used the lessons to get on in school. The boy kept his head down, did what he was told, and his life gradually improved. When he went to work at the local deli, he was able to buy newer clothes, and after a tormenting few years as an adolescent, he emerged in high school as fairly presentable. He was quiet, perhaps exceptionally so, but he was also dutiful and respectful. The teachers loved him, his "Yes, Ma'ams" and "Yes, Sirs," and the students warmed to his shy smile and growing charm. He had also become very, very good-looking. The boy always hid his family life, of course, along with his anger and the special skills he had acquired. In all those years in school he secretly knew he could have creamed any of those bullies or wiped the smirks off the faces of those silly girls with his secret knowledge. All this the boy kept locked inside. Back then he was afraid in ways he was not now. Knowing how to kill, knowing that he could kill, gave him great strength. To know he held the life of another in his power was what kept him going. ✤

✤ The man wiped his brow with his sleeve as the afternoon was warm, but a gentle breeze rustled the turning leaves of the trees and snapped the flag in the middle of the open green sward. He walked slowly over to the campanile and leaned casually against its yellow brick, cooled by the shade of the huge trees surrounding him. He lit a cigarette and closed his eyes.

These privileged brats don't know what life is all about, he thought. Some day . . . ✤

✤ His old man blew his brains out during the boy's senior year of high school. But that wasn't all that big a deal because by then he was really a young man and was capable of making his own way. In fact, it had been sort of a relief not having to please someone else every minute of every day. But his father had given him his hate, his sense of racial pride, and his belief that they were the chosen ones, the ones to rule. Even if his dad had blown it, the young man knew that he himself was destined for greatness. His grades got him a partial scholarship to one of the state universities, and he did fairly well, well enough to get his first real job in the computer field. He had always been interested in mechanical things, probably because at such an early age his dad had let him play with the many guns in the trailer, and later take them apart, clean them, learn to use them for what they were intended. By the time he graduated from college he had also learned how to use his looks and his winning smile to help him get what he wanted, especially from girls. But it wasn't until he held his first job that he really learned how to turn on the charm. ✤

✤ The man watched as a couple walked along a tree-shaded sidewalk. They were completely engrossed in one another, arms around each other's waists, a world unto themselves, completely unaware of anything going on around them. He felt revulsion. He thought about Chris.

His power over women started in a small way. The females at work were more aggressive and assured than at school and they were more willing to help him. At first he just asked for small favors: doing some last minute xeroxing, after-hours typing, or picking up his increasing workload. But then he discovered he had real attraction, animal attraction that women responded to, and the on-the-job favors turned into extracurricular sex. His success with the female office help became something of a legend.

Most of his conquests were simple, uncomplicated, and entirely physical. But the law of averages finally caught up with him when he began to see Chris, one of the keyboarders in the personnel department. At first she was like the others, only interested in the sex, but gradually she began to change. She baked him things—brownies, cookies, once even a birthday cake—and she began to offer to iron his shirts and do other little domestic chores. From the beginning of the affairs he had made one cardinal rule: he never took anyone back to his place. It was a sanctuary where he kept his collection of weapons and where he could relieve the tensions that living a double life created. But Chris got his address from the personnel files and dropped in on him unannounced one evening with take-out Chinese and a bottle of wine. He had to let her in; it would have been odd if he hadn't, but the evening proved to be a disaster, and a turning point in his life.

Chris immediately sensed something about the apartment was amiss, not in keeping with the person he was at work. He knew her intuitive reaction threatened his secret self. At first, he tried to laugh off the guns and Nazi gear by claiming they were an inheritance from a relative, a former World War II vet who was a collector. But he could tell from the start she wasn't buying it. After that night her behavior changed: she avoided him and wouldn't answer his phone calls. He knew he was in deep, deep trouble. All the fear and vulnerability he had so carefully worked to conceal was in danger. The headaches began again, and he knew she had to go.

Her murder and the disposition of the body were easy. She was missed at work, of course, but employees came and went in the highly competitive computer business and at first nobody seemed particularly concerned. When her landlord went to the police, however, things began to heat up. They swarmed all over the company offices, questioned her friends, pried into the personnel files. He realized it was only a matter of time before the cops would zero in on him. So he cleaned out his bank accounts, packed some essentials from the apartment, and vanished. ✤

✤ The man watched students sitting on the lawn eating their

lunches, studying, or sleeping with open books over their faces. Someone whistled at a dog that had gotten away from its owner and was dragging a limp leash behind it as it sniffed the ground. A chipmunk scurried in front of him, stopped, looked at him and, unafraid, scuttled into the bushes. "God, I hate all this," he muttered. "What a crock of superficial crap." He ground the cigarette butt into the ground, and turned away. ✤

✤ For years he wandered from city to city across the country, never staying for long in any one place and always living on the fringes. He remained anonymous, alone, and wary. The time was good for him. He developed more self-confidence and came to realize his old man had been right about everything. America had become corrupt, defiled by non-whites, prone to pettiness, absorbed in commercialism. The country needed a strong leader, one who would scourge it of its weakness, provide it with direction, give it a vision of purity and purpose, take it back to its roots.

During those lost years he spent his solitude nurturing his ambition, developing a plan of action, and when he was ready he changed his name, got into graduate school, and re-emerged in society associated with an institution which proved a perfect cover for his desires and a launching pad for the ambitions he was ready to further using whatever means necessary. ✤

✤ As he stepped away from the bell tower, he saw the front of Beardshear Hall, the main administrative building at the university, newly hung with patriotic bunting, red, white, and blue swags, and American flags. The Republican candidate for governor, Edward Van Der Boomsma, was giving a speech that afternoon. Workers were swarming all over the area checking the microphone levels, arranging chairs, and, at the last minute, stapling onto the platform election posters with Boomsma's rosy, round-cheeked, grinning face. The man stood in the lee of the campanile and carefully surveyed the campaign preparations. "Stupid sycophants, hangers-on, groupies," he growled. "Bunch of parasites." ✤

✤ The man still couldn't quite believe how easy it had been to become a political candidate in this year's gubernatorial race. All he had to do was make his desire to run known to a few people, subtly, of course, and without seeming too eager, and let them circulate a petition and bring the local party leaders in behind him and here he was. He was amazed at how politically useful his talent for secretiveness, his charm, his good looks, and even, oddly enough, his skills at killing people, were. People trusted him. He was the perfect candidate. And he could win, he was destined to win, and shortening the field of candidates was helping things along. With Boomsma out of the way, his path would be clear. The rest of the candidates were so iffy that his name would surely, this time, soar to the top of the list. Run-of-the-mill politicians were so stupid, so gullible, so vain, so weak, he mused. Bob Blackwell's death had been a piece of cake once he got that pudgy Melissa to lure old Bob into the woods. She had been like all the others, so easy to flatter into doing what he asked. He popped the bozo from a couple hundred yards; Daddy would have been proud. That Latina bitch folded the minute he bashed her on the head with the stone. Getting that dim-witted Woodward to off Vance was risky, and his bumbled attempt to cover his tracks was sloppy: Daddy would not have been proud of that. But Woodward probably would not come out of his coma, so he felt pretty safe. Only one more loose end to tie up and the organization would have served its purpose. He almost hated making Melissa's little girl an orphan. ✤

✤ The man walked out from the shade of the trees and slowly drifted across the grass of the central campus. His eyes never

stopped scanning the surrounding buildings. Looking high up
at the facades and rooftops, he seemed to be searching for something. Spotting what he was after, a smile slowly spread across
his face as his eyes riveted on an open third-story window in
Curtiss Hall directly across from the speaker's platform on the
steps of Beardshear.

Bingo. What a perfect spot, he thought. He remembered his
old man always said the first rule of a good sniper was to have an
open field of fire, and the second was to have an escape route.

The man had been all through the campus buildings surrounding the central campus. He had checked them out weeks ago, and
there was a rear entrance to Curtiss that led past East Hall to a
parking lot down the hill where he could stash a car. Blam, blam
and he'd be out the back and gone before anyone realized where
the shots had come from. Perfect.

He could just imagine it. The bunting and flags fluttering in
the afternoon breeze, the crowd eager to hear the front-runner.
After the fulsome introduction by some local politico, the applause and patriotic music would be piped in over the sound system with Boomsma smiling and waving to the crowd, shaking
hands with the platform dignitaries. Then before the noise quieted down, the candidate's head would explode, just like
Kennedy's in Dallas. Curtiss Hall might rank in Iowa history with
the Book Depository Building. Maybe there would even be another Zapruder in the crowd to catch it all on tape.

The man moved purposefully toward the classic limestone
building across from Beardshear. There was urgency in his step
and he was softly whistling through his teeth.

He remembered, just before I squeeze the trigger I must ask
God's blessing to guide the bullet on its true path—just like Daddy
taught me.

CHARLES L. P. SILET *has been writing about and reviewing mystery fiction and interviewing crime writers for the past dozen years.* He teaches courses in film and contemporary literature and culture at Iowa State University in the Department of English. *His most current books are:* Talking Murder: Interviews with 20 Mystery Writers *(1999) and* The Critical Response to Chester Himes *(1999). His* Oliver Stone: Interviews *were published in the fall of 2000.*

14.

Beelzebub—The Father of Lies

By Father Brendan Freeman

Carrying his case, the man entered Curtis Hall. No one paid him any attention. A couple looked at the case he was carrying, but thought nothing of it. A campus security guard gave him a cursory glance, but moved on. Shifting his case to make it not so conspicuous, he headed for the third floor window. He avoided the elevator and found a back stairwell. As he climbed the steps, he realized he was fulfilling a dream he had: to do Daddy one better. Lee Harvey Oswald had been given the main assignment in Dallas, but Daddy was one floor below as a backup, and Willard was on the grassy knoll just by the motorcade. Daddy just hid in the Book Depository Building until all the commotion was over and then reported to headquarters. Willard was never seen again. Headquarters claimed the Feds got him. Thank God they got to Oswald before he could talk.

Now it was his turn. After he killed Chris, he had kept moving and covering his tracks. That was more than 5 years ago, and he felt relatively safe now. However, he knew he had to keep his guard up at all times. During those years his hate had grown. He saw what was happening to America. His father fought to preserve the American way of life. Now, look at it. Immigrants were taking over everything. Blacks were equal to whites. Gays were in the government. The government! He especially hated the government. But, all this was pent up anger and frustration until he met Roger. ✤

✤ On the third floor of the Curtis building he found the room he was looking for. It was an abandoned office. It offered a perfect view of the Van Der Boomsma stage. It was a couple of hours before the rally was scheduled to begin. He lit a cigarette and waited. Time was on his side. He began thinking his dreams were finally in motion and that so many years of frustration were now finding outlet in action. He thought of Roger and their chance meeting a few years ago that had changed his life and opened up so many secrets of the past. He thought of all the planning and meetings finally coming to fruition. Roger was an old man now, but the fires of truth still burned in his eyes. He told him that the revolution started with the assassination of Kennedy was still going on.

The Army of God was alive and about to march again after so many years underground. The soldiers of God now realized they couldn't overthrow the government by force alone: killing the President had got them nowhere. Their new approach was to infiltrate the government and draw up and pass new laws that would stamp out gay gains and put blacks in their place. When Roger spoke about these people, he seemed to burn with fury. "God has a proper order for the world," he said, "and we have destroyed it. Everything is upside down and it's up to us to set it right. Remember, evil has no right."

Roger spoke of the young man's father, calling him a great freedom fighter for putting his life on the line in Dallas: "If we succeed in getting the governor's seat in Iowa, even if we have to kill to do it, we can slowly work our way across the nation. Who would suspect Iowa as the place to restart the revolution? Remember, evil has no rights and these people are evil." ✤

✤ He thought of these words as the crowd assembled to hear Van Der Boomsma speak. His adrenaline was pumping now. His whole body seemed to tingle: he was getting aroused. He knew it was time to kill. He opened his case and assembled the rifle, positioned himself and braced the barrel on the sill. His eye pressed against the scope, he zeroed in on the man at the podium. He whispered a silent prayer and squeezed the trigger.

Pandemonium broke out in the crowd. He didn't wait to see if he scored—in a flash he was out of the building and driving away. He couldn't wait to see the 5:00 news. He headed for the motel and Roger's next assignment. ✤

✤ In Iowa every vote counts. It's not like Illinois where Chicago can control the whole state. No single city controls Iowa. The candidates have to reach out to all the constituents. In Northeast Iowa there are a lot of religious institutions, and the people who support them are known to be faithful voters. Many candidates suddenly drip with piety when addressing them.

At New Melleray Abbey outside Dubuque, the Abbot of the monastery decided to invite one of the candidates to address the community. They were celebrating their 150th anniversary and the Abbot thought a little change would be in order. Since a priest was running for governor, he contacted Father Metterschmidt and invited him to speak to the monks.

This was not entirely new. Terry Branstad had paid a visit before his first election. He wanted to capitalize on the fact he had been taught by the Abbot's brother-in-law at Drake. When Branstad won, some of the monks claimed it was the power of prayer. Others said, "Well, I prayed he wouldn't win." This resulted in a long discussion on how God hears prayers that degenerated into a liberal/conservative argument about how someone can be pro-life and pro-capital punishment at the same time.

The Abbot made the announcement at a Sunday Chapter

meeting. "As you know, Father Metterschmidt is running for governor on the Reform ticket. He will be here in early September to talk to us about his platform. Are there any questions?"

Some of the monks were skeptical about a priest being involved in politics, but they kept their counsel to themselves.

Father Malachy raised his hand. "What diocese does Father Metterschmidt belong to?"

"I think he is a member of Domus Dei," the Abbot answered. "They are an exempt congregation, not under the jurisdiction of any bishop. They have a lot more freedom this way."

Father Ambrose spoke up. "I have been trying to find out something about his background on the web, but there isn't much available. Does anyone know anything about him?"

Silence. The Abbot finally said, "Well, Father Ambrose, why don't you ask him when he comes. We would all be interested, I'm sure."

Brother Martin raised his hand, "Are we going to invite the other candidates? It doesn't seem fair to hear from only one side."

The Abbot thought to himself, God, with all the media attention on this election, the last thing I want is a candidate getting shot on our monastery grounds. He answered, "No, this will be the only candidate. After all, Father Metterschmidt is a priest, and we have to stick together." He could see some of the monks didn't like this answer, so he closed the meeting with the usual prayer. ✤

✤ Outside the sky was a deep blue and the trees still as statues. The rays of the sun were coming at their morning angles highlighting the green, making them brilliant lime and dark olive with a touch of gold. Everything was still as a new day was being born. The violence in the world—in Iowa—seemed light years away. Life seemed to come to a whisper and a hush.

The phone broke into the Abbot's reverie. He hesitated to answer it. It was such a beautiful morning to watch the sun reveal all the hidden dark places in the trees. He picked up the phone. It was the guest master. "You have two visitors from the IDCI to see you."

"What is the IDCI?"

"I don't know; let me ask." The guest master turned to the visitors. "The Abbot would like to know: what is the IDCI?"

Michelle Dean smiled, while Bill Haldeman grimaced. "We are special agents with the Iowa Division of Criminal Investigation."

The guest master stiffened and turned a little pale. Dean was used to this. It used to tickle her to see the reaction of ordinary citizens when she showed her badge. Immediately they got serious and looked guilty. "We are here in regard to Father Metterschmidt's visit. We are his bodyguards for the day."

"Oh, thank God. I thought something was wrong," the guest master said.

There is something wrong, thought Haldeman. Don't these guys read the papers? There is a serial killer loose, and this guy is relieved one of the monks didn't get a speeding ticket. Besides, he was ticked off he and Dean were going to have to spend the night in the monastery guesthouse on a Saturday. No television and the Cardinals were playing.

Dean said she was looking forward to it. "It will be good for you, Bill. Clear your head; get you back on the right track."

"What do you mean, right track? I never knew I was off the track."

"Hey, kind of touchy, aren't we?"

"I guess so. It's just that I was looking forward to being a couch potato and watching McGuire hit his 50th homer. That's all. Nothing personal."

Nothing personal. Dean wondered about that. He was starting to grow on her, and she was looking forward to being with him without the usual distractions. Just time to talk and think and see what he was really like. Yeah, she was looking forward to it. She could see he was a little jealous of her crush on Father Metterschmidt—make believe though it was. She had gotten into the habit of calling him Father What-A-Waste. This always got a rise out of Haldeman. The first time she used it, he said, "What's that mean?"

"You know, he went into the priesthood: no dating, no marriage, what a waste!"

"Oh, stuff it," Bill said.

The guest master came back with the Abbot. After introductions, they went to a parlor to talk. Haldeman began. "Excuse me, but what do I call you?"

"Anything but late for dinner," the Abbot said, thinking he was clever.

Dean, who was Catholic, interjected, "Father, we have the assignment to protect Father Metterschmidt. As you know, there have been several murders connected with this election. Since Father Metterschmidt will be speaking to your community early Sunday morning next week, we feel we should stay in the guesthouse the night before. Is that okay?"

"Sure," the Abbot replied. "We have accommodations for married couples now."

Dean blushed slightly. "We are not married, Father."

"Oh, I see. Then we will arrange separate rooms."

"Thank you."

"You don't think there will be any trouble, do you?" the Abbot asked.

"No, Father, we don't, but we have to be careful," Bill said. ✤

✤ A week later, Dean and Haldeman arrived with their overnight bags. They had been talking all week about the strange places their jobs took them, but they never thought it would be this bizarre: a night in a monastery. Bill was on edge, not knowing what to expect. Dean was delighted she had him at a disadvantage. She had made a retreat before and kind of knew what it was all about.

After the guest master showed them their rooms, they went out to canvass the grounds. Dean fed Bill's anxiety with outlandish tales of chains being drug through the halls at night and churlish laughter coming from unknown sources. She was having a jolly time of it until Haldeman turned to her and said, "Why did you blush when the Abbot asked if we were married?"

"I didn't blush," she lied, but she was more subdued as they walked around.

After supper Michelle got Bill to go to the Abbey church to hear the monks chant Compline. Not being a religious kind of guy, he was, nevertheless, deeply moved by the chant.

After Compline, they met in the coffee room with the Abbot to plan the next day's events. It was simple enough. Father Metterschmidt was due to arrive at 7:30 a.m. He would speak to the monks, take a quick tour of the monastery, and depart. After the Abbot left, Dean and Haldeman sat drinking coffee. Bill's mood was changing.

"What's the matter, Bill?" Michelle said gently.

"I don't know. At first this place spooked me, but now I kind of like it. Not that I want to stay or anything like that, but it makes me think. You know, I really would like to be married someday, but the type of work we do doesn't leave much time for social life."

"Yeah, tell me about it," Dean said. As they talked, they realized that for all their time spent together, they really didn't know each other. In fact, they hid from each other. Now in this environment, the floodgates opened and they began to talk about a wide range of topics. Like shy deer, their real selves were flitting in and out of the thickets of their conversation. Ever so slowly, their defenses were abandoned, and they shared their dreams about the future, some of the hurts from the past, and what they really thought about each other. It was past midnight when they finally went to their rooms. ❖

✜ The next morning they were in front of the guesthouse when Father Metterschmidt drove up. He was alone, which seemed strange, since this would have been a good photo opportunity, Bill thought.

The Abbot greeted Father Metterschmidt and brought him into the Chapter Room to meet the monks. Dean and Haldeman stood guard. The monks were surprised at the Father's youthful, athletic look.

"Fathers and Brothers, I am happy to introduce Father Metterschmidt. As you know, he is running for governor of our state." The Abbot turned to Father Metterschmidt and said, "I want you to know, Father, we take our civil duties seriously here in the monastery. In a democratic society voting is extremely important and blah, blah, blah."

No one was listening to the Abbot. He always used these occasions as an opportunity to teach the monks, constantly misconstruing the appropriateness of the occasion. This irritated the monks no end.

When Father Metterschmidt finally got to speak, he went right to the point. Picking up on the Abbot's form of address, he began, "Fathers and Brothers, here I can speak freely, knowing you will understand. The time has come to do away with the separation of Church and State. As leader of the Christian Reform Party, I'm calling on all Christians to put this state back into its proper relationship with God. When we can no longer have prayer in our schools, when our children are bussed across the city because of a quota system, when immigrants are taking our jobs, it's time to instill good Christian values into our government. To do that, we have to demolish the wall between Church and State."

He went on to suggest religion had become subservient to the state, and he outlined a ten-point program to reverse the situation. "Government should be the handmaid of religion and not vice versa," he concluded.

As the Abbot looked around, he could tell the monks weren't buying it; some even looked alarmed. After a few questions, he hustled Father Metterschmidt out the door for the promised tour. Dean and Haldeman joined them. For some reason they looked different, the Abbot thought to himself. Must have been the long night's sleep in the guesthouse. ✤

✤ After the tour, Metterschmidt was history, though he left the monks sore amazed with much to talk of as the Indian Summer unfurled. Dean and Haldeman left, and the monastery returned to its normal existence. But not for long. A few days later, the Abbot was called to the guesthouse. As he approached the porter's office, he saw a young woman and a small girl waiting by the desk. The guest master said the woman asked to speak with the Abbot. She looked extremely anxious and frightened.

When the Abbot approached, she didn't wait for an introduction, but blurted out, "I need to talk to you, Father."

"Sure," the Abbot said. "Let's go down the hall to a parlor."

The little girl tagged along, caught up in her own world. The room was spacious enough with five comfortable chairs for visitors. As soon as they sat down, the woman said, "Father, I need to go to confession."

"Fine," the Abbot said, "but maybe we should take your daughter next door to the gift shop. What is her name?"

"Amy," the woman said.

"Amy, would you like to look around our gift shop while your mother and I talk?"

"Okay," she said.

The Abbot took her to the gift shop where old Brother Columba would tell her stories and keep an eye on her. When the Abbot returned, he assured the woman Amy would be safe with Brother Columba. "They are just in the next room. Now, what is on your mind?"

The words tumbled out. "Father, my life is so mixed up. Amy ... they are trying ... I have done terrible things, and I want to get out and get help."

"Wait, wait," the Abbot said. "Slow down. Take a deep breath and try to relax. Let us just be silent for a minute and say a quiet prayer."

Melissa tried to relax and collect her thoughts. After a minute or so she began, "I was raised a Catholic, but moved away from the church. I am in deep trouble, Father, and need help. I don't know where to turn. I have done some awful things. I want to start over, Father, and make a general confession and then move out of the state where my child and I will be safe. They will be after me."

Before she could begin her confession there was a loud and urgent banging on the door. Brother Columba burst in and cried in a panic, "The little girl is gone."

Melissa jumped up and ran past the brother.

The Abbot tried to calm Brother Columba and asked, "What happened? How could she be gone? You were with her, weren't you?"

"I went down to the storeroom to get some children's books for Amy. I was only gone a few minutes. She was looking at all the rosaries and medals. When I came back, she was gone. I looked around and ... nothing. She's vanished!"

The Abbot went to the gift shop and then took the sobbing Melissa to the porter's office. The brother porter had just come down from cleaning some guestrooms on third floor. He said he hadn't seen any little girl anywhere.

Melissa was sobbing, "My Amy, my Amy. Oh, God, why did I do this?"

The Abbot tried to calm her by saying, "I'm sure she just wandered off and is probably on the front lawn somewhere. Let's go look."

They went outside and saw nothing. By now Melissa was beside herself. The Abbot ran back into the guesthouse and called 911. Five minutes later two sheriff's cars pulled up and, after a thorough search of the guesthouse and grounds, put out a missing person bulletin.

Within an hour, Michelle Dean and Bill Haldeman were on the scene. They had been in Dubuque following Father Metterschmidt. Dean went to Melissa while Haldeman began questioning the Abbot. "Mr. Abbot, tell me what happened."

"Well," the Abbot said, "I was told there was a young lady just arrived in the guesthouse who wanted desperately to talk to a priest. Since I was free, I went over and here was this young lady with her little girl. She wanted to go to confession, so I suggested that the little girl, Amy, could go to the gift shop and Brother Columba would watch her there. The lady was reluctant, but I assured her she would be safe. I feel terrible about this."

"What did the lady say to you?"

"She said she had done some terrible things and wanted to change her life. Before she went to confession, however, Brother Columba interrupted us. That's all I know, officer."

Meanwhile, Michelle Dean was questioning the distraught mother. "Melissa, if you want us to help get Amy back, you are going to have to stop crying and tell me what happened."

Melissa wiped her eyes and looked at Dean. "I can't say anything until Amy is safe. They will kill her. I know they will. They keep saying evil and wrong have no rights. If I change, I will be evil to them, and they will kill me and Amy."

"Melissa, who are the 'they' you refer to? Is someone after you?"

"I can't say. I want Amy. I want my child back," she sobbed.

"Melissa," Dean said, "now listen to me. If we are going to help you, you have to cooperate. I saw you around a lot of the candidates. Is there some kind of plot going on here? Melissa, what do you know? Who is killing these candidates? Is there a conspiracy?"

"I can't tell you," Melissa said. "They will kill my Amy."

Michelle left Melissa to find Haldeman. She was sure there was some kind of conspiracy going on and needed to tell Bill. She ran into him by the gift shop. "Bill, I think we have a break in this case. Melissa is involved with some kind of group. I'm sure of it."

"Okay," Bill said. "The Abbot doesn't know much. Let's focus on finding the kid. If we can do that, I think we will unravel the whole thing. Once Amy is safe, I'm sure Melissa will sing."

FATHER BRENDAN FREEMAN *has been a monk of New Melleray for 42 years and Abbot of the community for 16 of those years. He has never written anything like this before and, if asked, will claim he knows nothing about this chapter. He is 62 years old and comes to Iowa by way of St. Louis, Missouri.*

15.

Anchor's Away

By Kathie Obradovich

Melissa was alone, hunched miserably on a straight-backed wooden chair in the Abbot's cell of an office. She had hardly moved for two hours except to reach blindly into the box of tissues in front of her on the desk and drop the used ones into the growing drift at her feet. The DCI agents, after 45 minutes of unsuccessful prodding and cajoling her for answers, had left her to stew after posting a guard outside the door. They had to race the lengthening shadows to cover the sprawling monastery grounds, looking for clues before the darkness swallowed them up. "How could I have been so stupid?" the young mother silently berated herself, over and over again. "Whatever made me think I could do this myself—and drag my poor little Amy into this mess with me?"

The little tune of self-doubt in Melissa's head was a golden oldie in the soundtrack of her life. Always a little chubby, with yellow hair and slightly startled, cornflower blue eyes, Mel had sensed when she was even younger than Amy that she'd never stand out in a crowd or reach the head of the class. Instead, she'd learned to get along with a bland but pleasant smile, a willingness to pitch in and help, to be the worker bee while someone else savored the honey.

Her sister, seven years older, had always been the beautiful one, the smart one, the one who met every day with the unswerving confidence that she could handle whatever it might bring. She had brought home straight A's, earned a scholarship to the University of Minnesota's business administration program, and landed a good job in the human resources department of a major electronics company.

Melissa had tagged after her big sister like a little mop-headed puppy as a child, and she continued the hero worship when Christine left for college. Mel's bedroom at home was papered with glossy magazine and catalog photos from the part-time modeling jobs Christine took for extra money but found too tedious to pursue as a career. To the shy seventh-grader, her sister was the symbol of everything she wanted to be: sleek, successful, and unafraid of anything and anyone.

Except for that day five years ago, when Chris had run into someone she couldn't handle. Her body, dumped nude and weighted with chains in a lake a few miles across the border in Wisconsin, had finally surfaced a month after she went missing. The police had never found the killer, although for a time they had hunted for a young man from her office that disappeared about the same time. A few co-workers thought Chris might have been a little sweet on the handsome, blond programmer, but none of them knew for sure.

In the months after Christine's funeral, their mother had sunk into despondency and a bottomless bottle of vodka. She died of an overdose of sleeping pills mixed with booze, which the coroner—a family friend—said was accidental. Melissa had found her mother's body. Her mother was clutching a photo of Christine, but had left no note for her. Melissa kept her suspicions to herself and collected the life insurance check. Her father had died in a car accident when Melissa was just a baby, so she was alone in the world at age 17.

Although she could afford to live off the insurance and the sale of the house for quite a while, she dropped out of school and landed a waitress job at a truck stop. She filled her days slinging greasy burgers and her nights swinging with seedy men—the kind of men who were drawn to her passivity and dim self-esteem like hyenas stalking a lame gazelle.

She was only mildly surprised to find she was pregnant and alone a few months before her 18th birthday, but she was absolutely shocked to discover the depth of her devotion to the wailing, red-faced stranger the doctor plopped onto her chest in the delivery room.

As little Amy grew from a cherubic, golden-haired infant to a precocious, azure-eyed sprite, the emerging resemblance to Christine began to shake Melissa out of her cocoon of lethargy and denial.

Numbed by shock and grief at the time of the murder, she had paid little attention to the details of the police investigation. But now, while Amy napped, she pored over yellowing articles about the crime her mother had carefully clipped from the *Star-News* and *Pioneer Press* and laid to rest in a shoebox. The metro newspaper articles were short on hard facts but long on heavy-breathing sensationalism. Each story was accompanied by sexy fashion shots of Christine, and most emphasized that her body had been found "totally nude." One writer even made a tasteless crack about the killer who "dropped Anchor in Wisconsin." The hometown paper had used Christine's high school yearbook photo and focused almost exclusively on interviews with stunned friends and neighbors who would never forget her.

Staring at her sister's dazzling smile, Melissa's despair and emptiness drained away and a wave of anger rushed in to fill the void. Someone had tossed away her beautiful sister, her best friend, like a piece of trash! And had gotten away with it —walked away scotfree while Christine was stuck in a box in a St. Paul cemetery. Melissa tore her eyes away from the pictures and scanned the text again, copying down the name of the frustrated police detective quoted most often, as well as the co-workers who had expressed their sadness and disbelief for the record.

Over the next few weeks, Melissa worked with a sense of purpose she hadn't felt since, well, ever. She cut her hours at the truck stop and used the time while Amy was at the babysitter to track down Christine's former co-workers and any friends who remained in the area. Those she was able to reach remembered little about Christine's last days or the mysterious co-worker who vanished, but they were so sympathetic that Melissa was emboldened to approach the police.

Detective Emil "Snookie" Schinker, a broad-faced Polish cop with 15 years on the job, glowered at first when he realized Melissa was there to ask questions about the unsolved case that had nagged him for five years. What he needed were answers. But the sight of little Amy in her cutest sunflower romper, trying to play peek-a-boo with him behind her mother's scarf, smoothed out the furrows in his square forehead and loosened his tongue.

Never dreaming that such a placid-looking little lady could be a budding vigilante, he told her his suspicions centered on an attractive 24-year-old programmer named P. J. Miller. "All the gals in the office were whispering that he and your sister were real friendly," Schinker said, waggling his black, bushy eyebrows suggestively and then doing it again, mugging at Amy as she chortled gleefully.

But Miller had vanished without a trace, cleaning out his bank accounts, leaving his apartment with nothing but a few coat hangers. "It was like he'd never existed—he was a cipher," Schinker said. "No past; name was prob'ly fake. Nobody in his office knew squat about him. Nobody had any pictures."

He shook his head. "There was a phone tip, three months ago." He hesitated, studying Melissa's face. She waited, keeping her expression carefully neutral.

"Some old broad," he continued, "from a pay phone in Waverly, Iowa. She said she'd seen a mope looked like Miller during a church service—kind of a tent revival—outside town. She'd seen a composite drawing of Miller in the *Star-News*, one of those "Most Wanted" things we had them print up, and she thought it looked like a guy who spoke at the service. She wouldn't give her name, but said she was worried the young man—she didn't get his name either—was trying to recruit local yoot into some kind of cult."

"Yoot?" Melissa asked, puzzled.

"Yoot. You know, kids. The young."

"Oh. Right."

"Yeah. So anyway, I drove down the next day, but they'd packed up the tent and skedaddled. Nobody knew where. I never did find them, but the local newspaper editor gave me a flyer that someone had dropped off about the rally. It had a funny-looking cross, and the name Army of God."

It took another year and a half before Melissa found the Army. Eighteen months of road trips to small-town libraries in Minnesota, Iowa, and Wisconsin, scanning through back issues of newspapers and using the library computers to search the Internet. The Army of God hadn't shown up on any cult websites, but it had made the community news page of the Lyon County *Register*. A rally and potluck were scheduled for the next weekend in Rock Rapids. ✤

✤ Shifting on her hard chair in front of the Abbot's metal desk, Melissa marveled at her foolishness. She hadn't even thought about calling Detective Schinker to pass on the Army's location. She'd just packed up her '95 Escort, strapped Amy into the child seat in back, and took off.

Joining the Army of God was even easier than getting pregnant, she thought ruefully. She looked just like all the other lost souls who were drawn into Father Phil's fold, and her natural talent for insinuating herself just took over.

Father Phil. From the first second she saw him, she knew he must be the one in the newspaper drawing. But a few seconds later, she wasn't so sure. Despite her efforts to remain cool and objective, just looking into his eyes began to confuse her thoughts. And listening to him preach—well, sometimes she could completely lose herself in his voice. He spoke casually but convincingly of his time in the seminary, his internships at small parishes. There was no way he could have been a cold-blooded killer in St. Paul, she told herself. He made her feel special, blessed.

Before she realized what was happening, she and Amy were irreversibly enmeshed in the Army of God. She did what came naturally—pitched in to help. And along the way, she found it easier to just ignore anything that might spoil her contentment. Things like the emerging themes of white supremacy. The secret, midnight meetings of the group's elders whom she never saw. The occasional, gun-shaped bulge in someone's jacket. The rumors of an "angel of death" who could take care of their enemies, and the never-mentioned disappearances of those who had "fallen from the way."

By the time the real nightmare began, when Bob Blackwell collapsed in a bloody heap at her feet, it was too late to turn back. She knew that now—but now they had her baby and . . .

Melissa suddenly sat straight up in the chair as if she'd been poked with a cattle prod. Her ever-present cell phone, which had been set on "vibrate," was buzzing in her pocket like a horsefly on meth.

"Yes," she answered, trying to sound strong. "I know, yes— No, I'm alone. They don't know anything—Please, I'm telling the truth!—OK, OK, yes—I will."

Melissa stabbed the "END" button and crept to the office door. She could hear voices just down the hall. No good. But the window was one of those modern crank-out models and it was only a short drop to the bushes. It was nearly dark by now. No cops were visible, but any second she expected a flashlight in her face and a rough "What are you doing!" Her heart was pounding as she slunk through the shadows, slipping into the cover of the woods as she made her way to the gravel side road a half-mile away, where they told her to meet her ride.

As they sped down U.S. 61 toward the interstate, neither Melissa nor her escort—a dour, heavily tattooed Illinois ex-con she knew only as Clem—noticed the black sedan that had pulled out of the cornfield behind them, keeping its lights off until it hit the traffic on the four-lane. ✤

✤ It was barely noon, but Lt. Scott Dallas's office in the gold-windowed Wallace Building was already a sauna. Actually, the time of day didn't matter—nor did it make a difference that his desk calendar said October. It was always sweltering in the Department of Public Safety's wing of the Wallace Building, winter and summer. The air-conditioning hadn't worked right for years, and it seemed the furnace ran overtime to make up for its lazy partner.

The Legislature had promised a brand-new public safety building a couple of years ago, with a spacious new crime lab for the DCI and updated facilities for the medical examiner. But when it came time to fork over the money, it seemed the legislators always found something else their constituents couldn't live without. Last year, it was a new sports arena and convention complex for Des Moines. The year before that, it was the infamous Gobi Desert habitat for Cedar Rapids.

But the heat that had been coming down on Dallas had nothing to do with the decrepit thermostat in the hall. The latest stack of newspaper editorials, with words like "bumbling," "Keystone cops" and "stymied" helpfully circled in red, were in his mailbox, courtesy of the department director's blue-haired secretary, Selma. Although he could have cheerfully strangled Selma, Dallas couldn't really blame the editorial writers. The murders of three gubernatorial candidates and as many near misses certainly seemed to warrant some visible effort at crime-solving by the authorities.

Unfortunately, the "authorities," at least the ones in the Division of Criminal Investigation, seemed to have no real authority in this investigation. "Ever since the President sent the FBI down to show us poor country cousins in Iowa how to do some Big Time Crime Fightin, I cain't even itch my arse unless Special Agent In Charge Harden shows me where," Dallas had complained, mimicking the head Fed's Southern-fried accent in a recent phone call to Haldeman. The weak attempt at humor failed to mask his frustration at once again having to explain to his top agents why they couldn't get off the candidate babysitting detail for even a day to work the case.

It was not that the Feds were sandbagging. They had swarmed over the investigation like a cloud of locusts, chewing up and digesting each and every detail. They were relentless, working day and night in the conference room and adjoining offices they had commandeered, apparently living on black coffee and carryout burritos from Raul's. They were sparing no resources, bringing in an accountant, the Internal Revenue Service, forensic specialists, a psych profiler, and a pair of secretaries. Dallas wasn't sure if the pimply teenage computer nerd was an agent or somebody's nephew. From what Dallas could tell, he spent all his time prowling political chat rooms and the candidates' websites, looking for weirdoes. Without exception, the federal agents were faultlessly polite, calling their hosts "sir" and "ma'am," while steadfastly refusing to tell them even the tiniest detail about what they were doing. They cordially hoarded every scrap of evidence, every lab report. Even the dead ends, dud tips, and cold leads were locked up tight.

Special Agent Verna Harden's first words to Dallas after "Howdy" were "Yer superiors have assured me I can count on yer complete cooperation. The first thang y'all need to know is that nuthin' about this here investigation will be released to the press except by me. The second thang y'all need to know is that I intend to release absolutely nuthin' to the press. And anyone else who does will be locked up for obstructing. Are we clear on that?"

Dallas had opened his mouth to suggest politely that he'd like to start investigating how far he could fit his size 11 wingtip up her bony behind. But before he could make a sound, he noticed his boss and his boss's boss were bobbing their heads in unison like the pair of Taco Bell chihuahua dolls in the back of his neighbor's Pacer.

It wasn't that he had that much sympathy for the media. It was rare but not unheard of for an investigation to be set back by the premature leak of information. But a complete news blackout in such a high-profile investigation was insane. The public, not to mention the politicians, needed to be reassured that the authorities had things well in hand, whether or not they really did. Besides, reporters abhor a news vacuum. They began filling their empty news hole with the criticisms of elected officials and concerned citizens who hadn't seen an inch of progress.

Even worse, for a while it seemed that Drew Wright from the *Register* was uncovering more clues than the cops. It was Wright, in a front-page story after Vance's murder, who revealed that the injured shooter, Rick Woodward, was also present in People's Park the day Bob Blackwell bought it. The two college students who found Blackwell's body, Shara and Zach, had confirmed seeing a man matching Woodward's description and Wright had seen him as well. Even though Dallas was certain the killer was on the roof of 12 Erlichman Plaza and not in the park, Woodward's presence—with a little girl matching the description of Amy Anchor—was significant.

A few days later, another Wright exclusive placed Woodward at the scene of the Lopez killing as well. This one was a little shakier. A few of the campaign staffers had noticed a scruffy-bearded man in a frayed "millennium" novelty T-shirt directing volunteers for the Metterschmidt campaign. Dallas knew a shirt with the words "Y2K ALL THE WAY" had been found in a guitar case Woodward had carried into the Hotel Fort Des Moines before shooting Vance.

Taking a risk that Woodward wouldn't regain consciousness and sue him for libel, Wright made a wild leap into speculation, suggesting that the Y2K message had prompted Lopez's dying words, "Happy New Year." It was thinner than Agent Harden's lips, Dallas thought. But it had the satisfying effect of making the public think the real killer was comatose in intensive care instead of out stalking the state's next governor. The unsuccessful attempts on Strong, Claridge, and Van Der Boomsma could be passed off as copycats—by everyone who didn't know the ballistics were a perfect match for the bullet that killed Blackwell.

Wright had assisted the investigation in another way, although he didn't even know it. After he printed a posthumous profile of Blackwell's shady business dealings, hundreds of outraged Republicans had buried the *Register* with letters, phone calls, and e-mail messages demanding that Wright be fired for defiling Blackwell's reputation. But the stories also prompted a Cedar Rapids plumbing contractor to drop a dime to the FBI. It seems Blackwell's construction company, which had won the general contract for building the $120 million, taxpayer-funded Gobi Desert simulation project, had been installing inferior materials and then padding its expense reports.

It was no secret Winston Claridge's Cedar Rapids computer

firm was working on the same project, developing the systems and software that would regulate the climate, handle the business procurement and accounting, and provide interactive educational kiosks for visitors. That much had been in the business section of the *Cedar Rapids Bulletin*. However, the FBI accountant and the IRS were convinced that the company, on the brink of launching a Midwest franchise operation, was raking in a lot more dough than Claridge and his lawyer could explain. For the past month the Feds had been chewing their way through Claridge's business records and personal financial data, letting him think it was an IRS audit but looking for motives for murder.

Dallas couldn't really buy Claridge as a killer, though. Even if you dismissed the potshot that nicked him at the Bix Fest as a fiendishly clever diversion, Claridge had solid alibis putting him at a dog show in Waterloo during the Lopez killing and judging a barbeque in Red Oak when Van Der Boomsma took a round in his bullet-proof vest at ISU. "Besides," Dallas told Harden, "the only Winston Claridge who's bright enough to plan and carry out a series of murders is the one who also likes to drink out of the toilet."

Of course, Dallas had not even found out about the Claridge theory until Haldeman and Dean had come up with a bargaining chip he could use to pry information from the Feds. His ace in the hole was Melissa Anchor—the one person who seemed to be connected to all the victims and half the suspects, too.

Once they started looking, it had been easy to tab Anchor as the chubby blonde honey that had lured Bob Blackwell to his rendezvous with death. The campaign manager, Homer McGruder, pointed her out in an old newspaper shot taken at a Blackwell ribbon-cutting, then later identified her from a photo Michelle Dean had snapped after Samuel Vance was killed. Dean had also pulled a fingerprint of Anchor's off a Kleenex box at the New Melleray monastery which Dallas expected would match the latent prints on Blackwell's body—not that the cursed FBI would ever confirm or deny that.

It was no coincidence Anchor had managed to walk away from the protective custody of a dozen cops at the Dubuque monastery. Haldeman and Dean, with permission from Dallas, had let her escape and then trailed her to a rundown farmstead in rural Marshall County where members of a clan called the Army of God had set up housekeeping.

Haldeman, who had lost the coin toss with his partner, holed up in an abandoned, rodent-infested corncrib just north of the farmstead. His team set up round-the-clock surveillance of the Army of God compound, secured warrants for phone taps and electronic eavesdropping, and settled in to watch and wait. The phone taps revealed that Melissa Anchor's daughter was alive, but she was being held somewhere else to keep Anchor from diving overboard. Unfortunately, the situation also kept the DCI from trying anything too aggressive for fear the child would be killed if anyone made a wrong move. Unless an opportunity arose to grab Amy and Melissa together, the agents would have to slap mosquitoes and lay in a good supply of rat poison.

Meanwhile, Dallas had asked the FBI team for help on tracing Father Metterschmidt's background. It was quickly established that the young "priest" wasn't really a man of the cloth—at least he wasn't really the "Phillip Metterschmidt" that had been ordained through the Davenport Diocese. The agents had tracked down the real Metterschmidt's ex-brother-in-law, the only relative who remained in the state, and confirmed that the late Father Metterschmidt had died of yellow fever after a missionary trip to Thailand.

Dallas assigned Agent Michelle Dean to shadow the phony Father. She had developed something of a rapport with him through a couple of chance meetings, the lieutenant noted. "Chat him up. See if you can catch him in a slip of the tongue," Dallas told her. He didn't notice that Dean blushed at the mere thought of Father Phil's tongue.

"Be careful," Dallas continued his lecture. "I don't know if this guy is a murderer, but it looks like he may be hanging out with a pretty seedy crowd. I'd sure like to know if he'd really kill to be governor."

KATHIE KINRADE OBRADOVICH, *an Ames native, has spent many of the past 13 years hanging out with cops, politicians, and various other officials and writing down what they say. She's in her eighth year of covering life under the golden dome for the Lee Enterprise Newspapers: The Quad-City Times in Davenport, the Mason City Globe-Gazette, and the Muscatine Journal. Her stories also appear in the Waterloo Courier. She and her husband, Jim, live in Des Moines with a cantankerous 18-year-old cat that has been labeled "super-geriatric" by members of the veterinary profession.*

16.

The Race Heats Up

By Terri Willits

Special Agent Michelle Dean checked in with her partner one last time before leaving to tail the phony priest. As far as she could remember, this was the first occasion she and Bill Haldeman had ever quarreled about their assignments. Apart from his displeasure at being stuck in the ratty corncrib, he was upset she had rejected what he considered to be the sensible options for her assignment—covert shadowing, concocting another chance meeting, or tapping the false Father's telephones.

Michelle argued that if she were forced to follow the candidate unseen, she wouldn't be able to get close enough to hear anything useful. And if he made her, it would be impossible to pretend her presence was a coincidence, since they had met 200 miles away in Davenport. As for staging a third "accidental" meeting, there was no way to look believable after she had met him twice out of uniform in Davenport and then had been in uniform during his visit to New Melleray. She finally agreed to the phone tapping idea, but was shot down when she went to the courthouse to request a warrant.

"Are you out of your mind?" bellowed Judge Erwin. "I agreed to taps on the Army of God compound because your agency provided probable cause they were holding a kidnap victim. But a tap on a gubernatorial candidate's phone?" His small black bow tie bobbed against his Adam's apple like a spastic cockroach. "Do you want to turn this into another Watergate?"

The short judge made her sit in a chair so he could tower over her as he continued his rant. "So he's not really a priest, who cares? Leak it to the media and let them hang him out to dry. If I gave you people a tap warrant for every politician who lied about his past, we'd have the biggest damn party line in the country."

Following that pleasant encounter, she had returned to the farmstead with only one plan left. Bill grudgingly conceded, then told her to be safe.

"You, too," she said.

"Mick, I mean it."

Unable to tell if his voice was thick from emotion or from the floating corn dust that had smudged his blue suit and coated his brown hair, she touched his arm. "So do I."

She didn't look back as she wound her way down the dirt lane, eased onto the gravel road and followed it to the highway. Turning west toward Marshalltown, she recalled the first press conference held by Father Metterschmidt, Candidate X as she now called him, where he had announced his intentions.

He had been an unusual candidate right from the start. The first issue, obviously, was his position with the church. Years earlier, a nun had been elected mayor of Dubuque, but this was the first time Dean had ever heard of a priest running for governor. The second issue was his tie to the state of Iowa. Being a member of the order of Domus Dei, he answered to Rome, rather than to the new Davenport Diocese Bishop, who admitted in a newspaper interview that he knew little about the political priest. The third issue was the location of his campaign headquarters.

"I wish I could run this campaign from my hometown of Davenport," he had stated, "but I need to be closer to the capital, where I hope to make my home next January." Michelle had never figured out how a smile could be both confident and humble at the same time, but this man made it work.

"I cannot in good conscience locate my headquarters in Des Moines, either," continued the Father, "a city so full of sin. Instead, I plan to work from Marshalltown, the site of the Veterans' Home where the brave, loyal men and women who fought for their country can come for help in their times of need."

His charisma had blinded them all, herself included . . . momentarily. If he thought Des Moines was such a sin city, why would he want a job that would require him to live there?

As she raced down the highway, more questions raced through her mind. Did he really care about the veterans, or did he have an ulterior motive for establishing himself in Marshalltown? How could this phony priest have gotten away with his disguise for so long, and why would he want to? And what was the Army of God? What does Melissa Anchor know about its involvement in the killings and attempted murders? She forced her thoughts back to her current assignment, the phony priest. Melissa and the Army of God were in Bill's capable hands now.

Michelle felt a warm flush rise in her cheeks as she thought of Bill's hands. They were strong and precise while aiming a gun on the firing range or in the line of duty. They were firm and compassionate while giving CPR to the dying Carmelita Lopez at the edge of Lake Okoboji. And they were warm and sensual the night they explored Mick's body at the monastery, the night the monks thought the two agents were sleeping in separate rooms. As she reached Marshalltown, she forced the memory from her mind and focused on the job ahead.

As with most politicians across the state, Candidate X had situated his campaign headquarters in a vacant storefront downtown. She parked and entered a large room filled with desks groaning under the weight of computers and clipboards and stacks of paper. Boxes of campaign buttons and flyers were piled along the walls, in the corners, and under the desks. The smile that had caused her briefly to lose her head last summer beamed down from posters covering the walls.

"Can I help you?" asked a pretty young woman seated at the desk nearest the door.

"I'm here to help you," answered Michelle. "I'd like to be a volunteer for Father Metterschmidt's campaign." Her plan was to take the direct approach, since the candidate was sure to recognize her from their earlier encounters at NorthPark Mall and the Bix Beiderbeck festival. She could only hope he hadn't spotted her acting in her official capacity at Lake Okoboji, at the monastery, or tailing him during the Bix 7 Race.

"That's great. Father will be so pleased to have you on board. My name's Cindy. Can you type?"

Four years of college and 10 years on the force, just so I can type, Michelle thought. My mother would be so proud. "Yes, I can, but is Father Metterschmidt here? I'd like to say hello before I start."

Cindy's deep sigh indicated her annoyance at the request. "Well, we really have a lot of work to do preparing for tomorrow's debate with Van Der Boomsma and Claridge, but if you think you have to."

"Thanks, I'll just take a minute of his time."

The harried woman pointed to a door in the back of the room and returned her attention to the computer screen. Michelle tapped lightly on the door, then stepped inside at the brisk, "Enter." When Candidate X looked up from his desk, his gray eyes clouded over briefly, then glistened with attention. "Michelle, isn't it?"

"I'm surprised you remember my name," she answered, glad she hadn't opted for the third chance encounter.

"I remember all of those in my flock. What brings you here from Davenport?"

I'm not a sheep, she wanted to answer. Instead, she gushed, "I heard your speech at the Bix fest, and with that choir singing in the background and you talking about a brand new Iowa, and prosperity, well, I decided I had to be one of your Christian Soldiers." At the time, she had felt mesmerized by his words. Now, it took all her training to repeat them with a straight face.

"I feel honored. Not many from my hometown have come all this way to work on the campaign. I was just going to ask Cindy to deliver this," he said, pointing to a large box on the floor, "but since she's in the middle of a polling project, would you mind if I asked you to do it?"

The last thing Agent Dean wanted to do was to be sent on an errand, but she plastered a grateful smile on her face. "I'd love to—anything I can do to help."

She was irritated she hadn't been told about the upcoming debate. As soon as she finished this errand, she'd have to figure out a way to convince Cindy that she should be assigned to help at tomorrow's event. What better place for the killer to be than at a meeting of the three major candidates?

"It's a donation we're making to the Meskwaki Indian Settlement. It's about 15 miles east of here on Highway 30. You can't miss it. Herman Lone Wolf will be waiting for you in the casino there, next to the keno machines."

As he rose from his chair and stooped to pick up the box, Michelle let her purse slide silently off her shoulder, then pushed it under the desk with her foot.

He turned and set the box in her arms. "Don't give this to anyone but Herman, do you understand?"

"Sure, nobody but Herman."

Dean returned to her car, retrieved the keys from her pocket and set the box on the front passenger seat. As she drove away, she pulled a small electronic device from the glove compartment, extended its antenna, and placed it in her lap. She had only driven a few miles when she heard the phony Father's voice emit from the receiver. Judge Erwin had denied her request to tap the candidate's phones, but she couldn't help it if she accidentally left her purse in his office, a purse that just happened to have a bug in it.

"Drew Wright, please. Yes, I'll hold." There was a pause. "Father Metterschmidt here. I wonder if you'd be able to meet me in Marshalltown before lunch. I have some information I think you'll find of interest regarding the Meskwaki Indians." Pause. "No, I don't think it can wait until the debate tomorrow. And I am offering you an exclusive." Pause. "Fine, I'll see you in an hour."

Michelle puzzled over the information Candidate X needed to share with the newspaper reporter. Surely it couldn't be his magnanimous gesture of donating one pitiful box of—of what? She pulled over to the shoulder and opened the box. Inside were children's clothing and a tattered stuffed bear. Big deal.

Nothing else came from the receiver except the sounds of papers being shuffled until the casino came into view.

"What's going on?" the false priest's voice squawked from the box again. There was a pause. "She won't, huh?" Another pause.

Damn, Michelle thought as she pulled into the huge parking lot. Another telephone call. How could she know what was going on when she could only hear one side of the conversation? Cramming the receiver into her pocket, she grabbed the box and walked toward the casino. As she pushed open the doors, she heard the voice say, "It sounds like the pigeon and the roost have both outlived their usefulness. You know what to do."

All she heard after that was white noise, so she stepped into the building and searched for Herman Lone Wolf. She had just located the keno machines when she heard some loud rustling sounds emitting from the receiver, then nothing. Either the bug had quit working, or it had been found. An uneasiness crept over her, so she dropped the box on the floor, unhooked the cell phone from her belt and dialed Haldeman. When he didn't answer, she tried the command wagon stationed near the Army of God compound. Getting no answer there, she told herself not to panic as she redialed Haldeman. Again she heard that awful sound. The sound of nothing. ✤

✤ After watching the empty yard for hours, Special Agent Haldeman snapped to attention when four men and two women ran out of the front door of the dilapidated farmhouse and across the yard to the two cars parked near the pole barn. Neither of the women was Melissa Anchor. They piled into the vehicles and gunned away, making it only a few hundred yards down the dirt lane when the farmhouse exploded in a fire ball.

Bill dashed out of the corncrib and across the yard to the inferno. Screaming Melissa's name, he circled the house, checking for any openings in the flame. The front door seemed to be more clear than any of the windows, so he attempted to enter, but the heat of the flames beat him back. Ripping off his shirt, he ran to a watering trough next to the barn, doused the shirt, then held it over his head as he entered the front door.

Everything inside the house was white hot. A ceiling timber crashed down behind him just as he stepped into the kitchen. Through watery eyes he spied a terrified Melissa tied to a chair. When he tried to pick her up, smoke filled his lungs at the exertion, forcing him to drop the chair back to the floor. He fumbled with the ropes until she was loose and helped her to stand. His shirt was now steaming and it scalded her face when he wrapped it around her head. Both of them coughed and gagged from the smoke until the intensity of the heat forced them to their knees. Since he couldn't carry her, he pulled and dragged the choking woman while they crawled toward the doorway.

She collapsed in a heap just a few feet from the front entryway.

With one final push, he got her through the door where she was grabbed by members of the surveillance team. Before they could reach his outstretched hand, the floor gave way and he crashed into the burning basement. ✤

✤ Leaving the box where it lay, Michelle pushed past the casino crowd and ran to the parking lot. Everything was wrong. A candidate preparing for a big debate would not be concerned with donating a box of children's clothes to an Indian reservation. How odd that children's clothes would be delivered to a man standing in the middle of a casino. Her bug should not have quit transmitting. And Bill should have answered his phone. She wasn't sure if she was speeding back to confront Candidate X or to find Bill when the fire engines screamed past her and turned down the road leading to the Army of God compound.

Her decision made, she cranked the wheel and skidded onto the gravel road, unable to see due to the dust clouds billowing behind the fire trucks. Unsure where the dirt lane was, she drove until she heard the sirens peel off to the left, then followed the sound. At the end of the lane, she slammed to a stop just behind the trucks and ran toward a few members of the surveillance team huddled in the yard.

"Bill?" she screamed.

They shook their heads and pointed to the charred remains of the house, the front door now just a memory. Before she could react to this information, she heard a yell coming from the back yard.

"Over here."

She followed two paramedics around the smoldering building. In the back, lying just beyond the storm cellar door, was Bill. She forced herself to ask, "Is he . . . alive?"

"So far," one of them responded. "Now get out of the way."

Michelle stood by helplessly while the medics prepped him

and strapped him to a gurney. "I love you, Bill," she called to the still form. "I love you."

Michelle and the rest of the team stood stunned as he was loaded into the back of an ambulance, but she was snapped out of her shock when her cell phone rang.

"Dean here," she mumbled.

"Agent Dean? It's Drew Wright. Did I call at a bad time?"

She snorted. "No. What can I do for you?"

"I thought you should know. I just finished a meeting with Father Metterschmidt. He says he knows where Amy Anchor is."

The words pulled her out of her despair and propelled her toward her car.

"What? Where is she?"

"He says the Meskwaki's have her."

TERRI WILLITS *isn't sure if she's an attorney who writes, or a writer who practices law. She has written three stage plays, producing two of them with grants; was the story treatment writer and script consultant for the CBS movie,* The Disappearance of Nora; *and has published numerous short stories. Terri is a board member of the Mississippi Valley Young Adult Writers Conference and is currently writing a young adult novel.*

17.

Nearer My God To Thee

By Mark McLaughlin

"This is an outrage!" Chief Brian Hawksblood shook his head angrily. "I do not see why I am being subjected to this ridiculous questioning. We have nothing to do with these "Warriors," this Army of God you keep talking about." Though only in his thirties, Hawksblood had thick streaks of gray hair flowing through his thick black hair at the temples. "What is this? Do you think all Indians are killers? Savages? I'm an accountant. One of my clients runs a doll shop, for Christ's sake."

Michelle Dean shot a worried glance at Drew Wright. Then she said to Hawksblood, "We're not accusing you of anything. Really. We just want to get Amy Anchor back, and the only thing we have to go on is what Father Metterschmidt had to say."

Hawksblood stood up behind his metal desk, which had been painted dark green. Some of the paint was chipped, revealing older yellow paint underneath. Framed photos of smiling children and seniors—grandparents probably—were spaced on the floral pattern wallpaper. The accountant's office was cozy, Michelle thought. Friendly. Hardly the center of a supposed evil empire. "And where is this Metterschmidt?" Hawksblood shouted. "Don't I get a chance to meet the man who is making these accusations?"

Lt. Scott Dallas entered the room with two police officers following close behind. "I have some good news and some bad news, folks."

Michelle sighed heavily. "Please, the good news first. At this point, we need it."

"I just got off the phone with the hospital. Your partner Bill is going to be okay. He has a broken leg and arm, a few burns, but the man's lucky to be alive. Melissa's okay, too." Dallas's smile slowly turned to a grimace. "Unfortunately, the media has caught wind of this whole Meskwaki mix-up. Now the settlement is crawling with reporters."

"How did they find out?" Wright said. "Who told them?"

"Who else? Our old buddy Father Metterschmidt. He knows he's beaten, so he's trying to shift the blame and turn this whole fiasco into a media circus." Dallas settled into an overstuffed armchair. "At least that's my best guess."

A young Indian woman in a purple bathrobe entered with a tray of cups. "I figured you folks could use some coffee. Brian's the coffee expert in this house, but I—"

"That's fine, Lisa." Brian took the tray from his wife and set it on his desk. "Make sure the kids are all in bed. Tell them everything is going to be okay. They're not scared, are they?"

Lisa laughed. "Goodness, no. Tommy thinks this is an episode of *COPS*. He's using talcum powder to dust the bathroom for fingerprints. He's making a real mess in there, but at least he's not underfoot. Speaking of mess, those vehicles outside are driving all over the grass. The lawns around here are going to look like a battlefield in the morning."

Dallas walked up to Lisa. "Thank you for your patience. I realize we're disrupting things around here. I will personally make sure a team of housecleaners and lawn experts set everything straight after we're out of here. Even if I have to pay for it myself."

Hawksblood smiled. "Thank you. So I take it you no longer

think we're the kidnappers." He gestured toward the desk. "Well, we don't want that coffee to get cold."

Michelle picked up a cup and sipped the rich blend. Brian and Lisa were an attractive couple. It was a pity their evening had to be ruined with all this police business. They were the victims this evening—innocent pawns trapped in a game that didn't even concern them. She hoped neither of them would be hurt. And what about little Amy? The littlest, most helpless pawn of all. Even if Amy was still alive and they managed to rescue her, who would take care of the poor kid if Melissa ended up behind bars? Well, maybe if Melissa cooperated, a deal would be worked out . . . . No jail time, in exchange for a full confession.

She looked out a window, into the night beyond. Cars and flashlights everywhere. Dozens of people walking around— police officers, settlement residents, children. "This isn't good," she said. "I have a bad feeling about this. Really bad."

"What's on your mind?" Wright said.

"All these reporters . . . . I think we're being set up." She set her cup back on the tray. "My God, the other candidates."

Wright looked out the window. "Did you see them?"

"No, but I'm afraid I might," she said. "Candidates love reporters, and this place is becoming one big camera shoot."

Dallas jumped to his feet. "You're right. They're going to start dropping in, and that bastard Metterschmidt knows it. Excuse me, folks. I have to make some calls, though it's probably too late to stop them." He dashed out of the office.

Lisa took her husband's hand. "Are you making any sense out of this?"

Hawksblood nodded. "The candidates are all going to start showing up, just so they can get their stupid faces on TV. And that's when the shooting's really going to start." He turned to Michelle. "Isn't that right? More shooting, more lives. And who's going to protect my people?"

"You two," Michelle said to the officers who had entered with Dallas. "You heard . . . um . . . Mr. Hawksblood. Make sure all the folks living here on the settlement are told to stay indoors, away from any windows."

The officers bumped into each other as they rushed to the door, and jostled for a moment to see who would be the first one out.

"You must think we're a bunch of idiots," Michelle said with a tired, sad laugh. "It's funny. A moment ago, I didn't know if I should call you Chief or Mister. Is Mister okay?"

"Just call me Brian." Hawksblood put a hand on the agent's shoulder. "We're not worried about tribal etiquette around here."

Lisa gave her a wink. "Oh, he likes it when I call him Chief, though. But if he ever calls me his squaw, I'll hit him with my shoe. And honey, it ain't no moccasin. It's got plenty of heel on it."

Dallas returned to the office. "Yep. It's hittin' the fan out there. I've been told Louella is in the settlement community center at this moment, talking to reporters. She's a gutsy gal—and she sure didn't waste any time. I've got officers at all the entrances. I did manage to catch Claridge at home. He had no intention of coming here, which is good: one less candidate for me to worry about. Of course, with Louella here, that paints him as a no-show coward. That's no way to win."

"Unless somebody shoots all the other candidates," Michelle said.

Dallas nodded. "Good point. Michelle, let's get over to the community center. Brian, Lisa—for your own safety I think you should stay in here with your kids. I'll leave an officer here to watch over you, in case Metterschmidt gets any more crazy ideas and tries to come after the Chief."

Hawksblood brushed his fingertips lightly over his wife's cheek. "We still haven't watched that Disney movie we rented. Let's see if these folks can straighten things out before the movie ends." He nodded at Dallas. "Sure. We'll be upstairs if you need us. Just tell us when it's over. If you'll excuse us, it's time for us to introduce our kids to Mary Poppins." ❖

❖ In the community center, Louella Strong dug around in her purse until she found her high-fiber energy bar. "I practically live off these things these days," she said to the nearest reporter. "A woman on the go needs her fiber." Suddenly she laughed. "Go! Fiber! I wasn't even trying to make a joke. Well, if I don't win the election, maybe I can get into stand-up comedy."

Dallas marched up to the laughing candidate. "Louella, do you have a deathwish? What the hell are you doing here?"

The gray-haired woman took a big bite from her bar. Then, after giving it a thorough chew, she swallowed and smiled. "What do you want me to do? Cower in my basement? I've worked too hard to go into hiding." She eyed the nearest TV camera. "Iowa doesn't want a wimp for governor. Strong by name and strong by nature! If someone's going to shoot me, well, let 'em try! I've fallen off horses at least a dozen times. A tractor once almost tipped over on me. A boar hog sank a tooth in my thigh last year. Well, I survived all that and I'm going to survive this. When I found out the Meskwaki people were in danger, I rushed right over because they are my fellow Iowans!"

"Damn, she's good," Michelle whispered to herself. It was clear to her that the campaign trail had made Louella tougher and more outspoken than ever.

Louella tapped her finger on Dallas's sternum. "I haven't had more than twenty minutes of sleep in the last twenty-four hours, so maybe I'm a little punchy. But by God, I can't turn back now. I will not disappoint all the people who have helped me get this far."

She walked around the community center. Dozens of cameras followed her every move.

"Are you in here, assassin?" she cried. She grabbed her blazer by the lapels and fanned it open. "Kill me! Kill a middle-aged woman. Will that make you happy? Will that make you feel like a real big shot? Well, open your ears because I've got some head-line news for you! Are you listening? Then get a load of this: I refuse to be afraid. Do you hear me? I am an Iowan and I refuse to be afraid!"

For a moment, there was silence. Then Michelle heard some-one clapping. She was surprised to realize that it was—herself.

Soon everyone in the community center was clapping and shouting—even the police officers and the reporters.

"Ladies and gentlemen," Wright said to no one in particular, "we have a winner."

At that moment, an explosion rocked the settlement. ✤

✤ Dallas and Dean rushed out of the community center, Louella following close behind. Media helicopters circled overhead. Michelle found herself absurdly wondering what part of the movie was playing in the Hawksblood house right now. Were they watching the part where Julie Andrews and Dick Van Dyke jumped into the chalk drawing with those cute, sappy British kids? That was always her favorite part. If only she had a chalk drawing of her own to jump into. When all this was over, she was definitely taking a vacation. With any luck, it would be with Bill. Instead of a chalk drawing, how about a sandy European beach . . .?

She pulled herself out of her thoughts. She desperately needed sleep, but damn it, this was no time to start getting loopy. She saw that an opening had been blasted through the brick wall that stood along the northern border of the settlement. Media heli-copters were shining spotlights so that their cameras could reg-ister the action. Blood-red pickup trucks were driving though the opening, and in the back of the lead truck stood Father Met-terschmidt in a flowing white robe, Alan Fairfield in a red satin evening gown with a rifle hanging from one shoulder and a tacky silver purse swinging from the other, and Candy Fairfield in a pinstriped business suit, holding little Amy Anchor tight.

"Holy Mother of God," Wright said. "What do we have here?"

In the trucks that followed, men and women with T-shaped crosses around their necks tossed flowers in every direction. They also carried guns—and not just rifles. Michelle spotted plenty of machine guns.

Michelle then noticed Edward Van Der Boomsma standing by himself twenty feet away. No doubt he had just arrived. And no doubt he was terrified by the spectacle before him. The crotch of his pants was as wet as any crying baby's diaper, and a TV reporter had his camera aimed at the spreading stain. So much for that political career.

"The time for Truth is at hand!" Alan Fairfield cried. "God's Chosen Ones, His Army of God has come to deliver His ultimate message!"

"You tell 'em, Roger!" Metterschmidt shouted. "Tell the world!"

The lead truck stopped so abruptly that its passengers had to steady themselves against the cab.

"Two-party politics be damned!" Candy screamed to the reporters. "From this day forth, the word of God is all the politics anyone will ever need! T is for Truth and T is for Time! We shall rule humanity with Truth throughout all of Time!"

Time. Michelle thought about Carmelita's last words: Happy New Year. Time. Father Time. Father Metterschmidt . . . . A strange logic, but then Carmelita had just suffered a massive head trauma . . . .

Louella Strong marched forward, stumbling on some bricks that had flown from the explosion site. "The word of God? Says who? What kind of God asks His followers to go around terrifying people? Not my God!" She put her hands on her hips. "Look at all those guns. So much for your precious slogan, 'Violets Not Violence.' And by the way, who the hell is Roger?"

"This is Roger," Metterschmidt said, grabbing Alan Fairfield by the forearm. "He is the one who showed me the way, the glorious path to salvation. We are Warriors of God on a mission, and we cannot be stopped. Roger has been my father and my mother—my world, my everything—and he will be your everything, too. Whether you like it or not."

Michelle rushed up to Louella's side. "Please, this is not your battle."

"Like hell it isn't!" the older women cried. Reporters milled around, their cameras focused on Strong's glaring eyes. "I am not a vengeful woman by nature, but when people push me, I push right back! That's the Iowa way!"

"Then that way must be corrected," Alan said, nonchalantly raising his rifle. "With a deer slug."

"I've got a few words to say to you, mister!" Louella said. "That purse doesn't go with that dress, and your gun doesn't go with my plans to die at the ripe old age of one hundred and ten!" So saying, she picked up a brick and threw it with all of her might, just as Fairfield squeezed the trigger.

The slug hit the brick with a sharp crack. The brick split in mid-air, and a large chunk of it sailed off at an angle, right at Father Metterschmidt, hitting him in the face. A splash of blood spattered Alan's satin dress.

A crooked smile worked its way across Michelle's face. Yeah, club soda wasn't going to get that stain out. And prettyboy Metterschmidt—? Not so pretty now.

The priest moaned and fell out of the truck. Alan and Candy screamed and jumped to the ground to help their misguided follower.

Michelle rushed up to the truck and hopped in the back. She grabbed the trembling Amy and carried her away from the Fairfields.

"No!" Alan cried. "Not my lamb, my lamb, my special, glorious lamb! This can't be happening! Not now, not when we were so close!"

Michelle looked at the three tragic, ridiculous figures grouped by the side of the truck—one limp, one sobbing uncontrollably, and one looking nervously about. She had no idea what they thought they were close to, and she didn't want to know.

"I think I need another energy bar," Louella said to Wright two seconds before she passed out from sheer exhaustion.

Mark McLaughlin's *fiction, nonfiction, and poetry have appeared in almost 275 magazines, anthologies, and websites worldwide. These include* Galaxy, Talebones, Transversions, The Pinehurst Journal, Brando's Hat, The Zone, Palace Corbie, Bending the Landscape, 100 Wicked Little Witch Stories, *and* The Year's Best Horror Stories: XXI and XXII *(DAW Books). His most recently released story collections are* ZOM BEE MOO VEE & Other Freaky Shows *(Fairwood Press) and* I Gave At The Orifice *(Eraserhead Press). Three more McLaughlin story collections from other publishers are forthcoming. When not writing, Mark enjoys eating, breathing, and occasionally sleeping.*

EPILOGUE
Lokrum,
August 2003

By Susan J. Koch

They had spent a leisurely morning rambling hand-in-hand through the silent ruins of the Benedictine monastery on the eastern side of the island. And now, with the maestrale, the soft Mediterranean summer breeze, gently wafting her hair, Michelle Dean lay contentedly on a blanket of pine needles at the edge of the island wood. Just across the channel, the ancient Venetian city of Dubrovnik raised its limestone walls toward the brilliant blue of the sky as local fishermen navigated their tiny boats round the Fortress of the Passing Bell toward home. The only sounds were the soothing lap and suck of waves lost among the rocks and the deep, steady breathing of her husband sleeping peacefully beside her. What a year it had been.

It was now almost ten months since Bill had fallen through the floor of that burning farmhouse during his heroic rescue of Melissa Anchor. For Michelle, the weeks following that dreadful day had been defined by fear—fear that Bill would not wake up at all after surgeons pieced together his badly shattered leg; fear that he would never walk normally again; and fear that she had missed the only opportunity she would ever have to look the man she loved straight in the eye and tell him how much he really meant to her. But he did, and he would, and before she had had a chance to utter a word, Bill had opened his eyes to her anxious face and muttered: "What do you think, Mick?" And in that moment Michelle understood that all would be well.

As fate would have it, the surgeon who reassembled Bill's leg was orthopedist and bicyclist extraordinaire Robert Breedlove. Breedlove was known all over the state, not only for his surgical skill, but also for his yearly stunt of doubling the distance of the Register's Annual Great Bike Ride Across Iowa, fondly know as RAGBRAI, by racing the route both directions during the same July week when most of the 10,000 or so other riders held to a more sane and one-directional pace.

It was Breedlove's idea that Bill make cycling the core of his rehabilitation, and that was just the challenge Bill had needed. By early March, Bill's proposal of marriage included not only the customary engagement ring and a spectacular bouquet of Michelle's favorite "Amber Queen" roses, but also a gleaming new pavo-purple metallic Co-motion Speedster tandem bicycle with Air Bunz seats, Louis Garneau Globe bike helmets, matching jerseys, and two official passes for the 30th anniversary RAGBRAI—an enchanting package deal that no reasonable woman could possibly refuse.

Michelle had accepted with two conditions: the guarantee of a cozy, though transient, "bridal suite" each night of the ride and the promise of a second honeymoon week on a beach as far away from a bicycle as they could get. Amazingly, their now mutual friend, Lt. Scott Dallas of the Iowa State Patrol, who had visited Bill regularly in the hospital and later shared training rides with the couple throughout the spring, had quickly provided both! A few e-mail messages to old friends along the RAGBRAI route resulted in generous invitations (and assurances of marital seclusion) at each overnight stop. And one of Dallas's old friends from the Iowa Law Enforcement Academy, who, like several other

Iowans, had recently worked as a police trainer for the United Nations in the former Yugoslavia, suggested the couple spend a week in Dubrovnik, the beautiful stonewalled city on the Dalmatian coast now popular with international aid workers in the Balkans. With a little help from the Internet and a few e-mail messages to Croatian Airlines in Chicago, the trip was set.

Bill and Michelle were intent on their joint rehab goal of a RAGBRAI honeymoon, so Michelle's mother, Janice, had happily accepted responsibility for planning the wedding in Davenport. And so, on a warm July evening just a few days before RAGBRAI riders dipped their wheels into the waters of the Missouri River to begin a week's worth of sweat, sweet corn, and port-a-potties, Michelle and Bill were married in true Davenport tradition—under the arches in the rose garden of the Vanderveer Botanical Garden. Father Rudy from nearby St. Mary's Church, one of Michelle's former classmates from Assumption High School, officiated at the ceremony, and as she and Bill linked arms and joyfully turned to greet the world as husband and wife, they were surrounded by friends and family—both old and new.

The dozens of Barbara Bush roses blooming throughout the garden, though the most fragrant, had not been the only witnesses with political credentials. Governor Louella Strong had also been a most welcome and enthusiastic guest.

It's true, a few ultra-conservative nay sayers were still grumbling a half a year after Iowa's first woman governor had been inaugurated that Strong had literally won the election by the process of elimination: murder. Edward Van Der Boomsma, who had been the Republican front-runner after Bob Blackwell has been killed, had quit the race and disappeared from the Iowa political scene immediately after the humiliating television exposure of his less than heroic incontinence during the episode at the Meskwaki Settlement. Word in Iowa Democratic circles, though possibly unreliable, was that Ed had become the Iowa spokesperson for DiapersAmerica.COM, an online adult disposable diaper distributor.

With Van Der Boomsma's evanescence, it had finally become clear to the Republican leadership of the state that a "Vote for a STRONG Iowa," as Louella's campaign slogan stated, was their best bet to win the governor's office, and so, with only a few weeks left in the campaign, she had become the official Republican candidate. The fact of the matter was that most Iowa voters, mesmerized by the statewide news coverage of the face-off between Strong and the lunatic horde, were genuinely impressed by a politician with the courage to stand up to a gun-toting goofball like Alan Fairchild. Televised images of Louella Strong heaving the infamous brick had provided the kind of free publicity no public relations firm could have been paid to produce, and Strong was swept into office with the biggest margin of victory since Ray beat Schaben in 1974.

Claridge, as it turned out, found himself the loser of more that the election. *Des Moines Register* reporter Drew Wright, who had become suspicious early in the campaign of Claridge's reputation in the Cedar Rapids business community, had written a brilliant and devastating investigative series under the screaming headline "Politics is Murder" in the weeks following the election. Though the main focus of the series, which had won Wright a Pulitzer Prize for investigative reporting, had been the murders that had plagued the campaign, Wright also described numerous campaign finance violations in the Claridge camp, many of which had been masterminded by Candy Fairchild.

It turns out the opportunistic female had created a whole new definition of "running mate" when she had decamped from her husband's campaign and hooked up (in more ways than one) with Claridge. Just minutes ahead of an arrest, Claridge had hopped a plane to Guadalajara. Federal authorities were still on the lookout for both he and Candy, who had managed to avoid arrest at the settlement and was thought to have left the state with Claridge under an assumed name.

Poor Winston. Claridge's faithful, though ill-mannered, boxer was ignominiously abandoned in Claridge's car, parked illegally in the kiss-and-fly lane at the Des Moines airport. When the big-hearted Governor-elect Louella Strong heard the pooch was languishing unwanted under a death sentence at the Polk County Humane Society, she immediately adopted him and settled him in canine comfort in a spanking new doghouse at Terrace Hill, the governor's residence. Through this twist of fate, Winston became Iowa's First Dog.

The eruption at the Meskwaki Settlement had blown the lid off the Army of God, the pseudo-religious cult behind the Iowa campaign murders. After those many months of piecing together whatever sparse information they could gather, Lt. Scott Dallas and the Iowa DCI now had more evidence than they needed to uncover the modus operandi of the group and the chain of events that had brought such unprecedented tragedy and media attention to Iowa.

Former candidate and priest-impersonator Phillip Metterschmidt, his good looks ruined for good by a chunk of Louella Strong's brick that permanently relocated his nose left-of-center, was singing like a canary in the Polk County jail where he was awaiting trial on charges of conspiracy and murder. There was no question Metterschmidt himself was responsible for the murders of Robert Blackwell, who'd been shot early in the race, and Carmelita Lopez, who had been hit over the head with a rock and drowned in Lake Okoboji. As the investigation continued, it became clear the two political murders were the last of a long string of crimes Metterschmidt had committed and, with the help of Melissa Anchor, the Iowa DCI had also gathered enough evidence to charge him with the killing six years earlier of Melissa's sister, Chris. Metterschmidt proudly claimed credit for the killings as if he were counting coup, and when he wasn't imperiously demanding an audience with his "father," Alan Fairchild, who would surely explain everything, he spent most of his time serenading fellow prisoners at the top of his lungs with his personal interpretation of "Onward Christian Soldiers." There was some question as to whether he would be competent to stand trial later in the fall.

The real mastermind behind the whole nefarious conspiracy, of course, had been Alan Fairchild, who was also in jail and awaiting trial. Posing in Iowa for the past ten years as a chef and a model citizen had provided Fairchild, who had a long list of previous convictions as one Roger Burton, with the perfect cover. Burton had been a member of the Army of God sect since his teenage years in Oregon, where he had been thoroughly indoctrinated with their extremist political views and savage schemes for taking over the government. He had quickly recognized in both Metterschmidt and Rick Woodward, who remained comatose in a Des Moines hospital, the unstable but fiercely loyal disciples he would need to achieve his own violent ambitions to win the Iowa governor's race.

It was Melissa Anchor who provided the essential testimony that would eventually put Burton away for good. Having been reunited with her daughter Amy, safe and sound after the Army of God kidnapping, Melissa had worked willingly with Michelle Dean and other investigators at the DCI, recalling conversations, dates, meetings, and other evidence to help build the case against the group's leader.

It was Burton who had ordered the murders of Blackwell, Lopez, and Vance—as well as the attempts on the lives of Claridge, Van Der Boomsma, and Strong. He had also arranged the threats to Melissa at Backbone State Park (actually it had been Metterschmidt in bearded disguise who had tightened the rope around her neck) and, later, little Amy's kidnapping when the

Army's success was threatened by the fear that Melissa might defect.

What Burton hadn't counted on was that his own wife, Candy, would play him for a fool, pretending to go along with plans for the attack at the settlement when, all the while, she was literally in bed with that fat-assed computer geek, Winston Claridge. Even as he cooled his heels in jail, Burton still couldn't believe it, and thinking of Candy and Claridge together and living it up in Mexico made him want to scream.

Perhaps if any good had come from the whole demented succession of events, it had been the dramatic reversal in Melissa Anchor's fortunes. In exchange for her cooperation with the authorities, Melissa had been placed on probation and assigned community service. After hours of interviews and testimony, both Melissa and her daughter had worked their way into Michelle's sympathetic heart and Michelle's mother, recognizing another victim in need of rehabilitation, had practically adopted the young mother and her little one.

Janice had arranged for Melissa to do community service under her supervision in the Davenport Community schools and, by the end of the school term in June, Melissa had discovered she had a real knack for working with those goofy middle-schoolers. By the time Michelle's and Bill's wedding date arrived, Melissa had been accepted for the fall semester at the University of Northern Iowa where she would major in teacher education and minor in, what else, political science. Little Amy had been the perfect choice for flower girl, and she practically stole the show at the wedding when she walked solemnly down the aisle with a basket of rose petals on one arm and her much loved stuffed bear, Higgins, in the other. ✤

✤ Lazily drifting back and forth between daydreams and sleep, Michelle was awakened by the distant ringing of the angelus bells floating across the water from the church of St. Blaisus and by the delicious tickling of her husband's lips gently against her cheek. "Hey, partner, should we be getting back to the dock?" he asked, after a lingering kiss.

Several minutes later she responded with an entirely unconvincingly innocent look: "What do you say we walk back through the monastery grounds?"

They gathered their backpacks from under the trees and, arms entwined, headed slowly back up the trail.

"What is it with us and monasteries?" the woman mused.

"I'm not sure, but I think we're going to miss the ferry."

SUSAN KOCH *is originally from a small town in South Dakota. Her personal essays and poetry have appeared in* Lyrical Iowa, The Des Moines Register, *the* Waterloo Courier, *and* Northern Iowa Today. *She is currently at work on a historical novel,* The Ballad of Dora LaPine, *based on a notorious murder case that occurred in her hometown nearly a hundred years ago. During working hours, Susan is a Professor and the Associate Vice President for Academic Affairs at the University of Northern Iowa. Before contributing to this book, her only brush with politics had been singing "Up, Up and Away" for then-president Richard Nixon in 1968. Though the audiotape of this performance has, thankfully, disappeared, it is highly unlikely it would have been one of those subpoenaed a few years later by the House Judiciary Committee and, thus, she claims no responsibility whatsoever for Nixon's political demise. She wrote this chapter while on vacation in Dubrovnik, Croatia.*

WINSTON, THE CANINE: *Winston is short for "Shanley's Winston." When Mickey Zucker created the character of Winston Claridge in Chapter 1 and gave him a dog as a sidekick, KUNI News Director Greg Shanley couldn't resist the door to immortality this opened for his beloved family pet. It seemed written in the stars that Winston Claridge would have a dog named Winston.*

The real Winston, Shanley's Winston, is a purebred boxer who has several grand champions in his lineage. The Shanleys adopted Winston from a Cedar Rapids family just after he was born in the Spring of 1996. Shanley's Winston, perhaps like Winston Claridge's irrepressible pet, is big for a boxer. Most boxers weigh 45 to 50 pounds; Shanley's Winston hovers between 75 and 80. The dog is deer red in color with a soft black muzzle and a white chest and toes! His favorite snacks are apple cores and whatever else he can reach in the garbage.

Thus, Shanley's Winston shares several traits with his fictional counterpart. His most memorable hobbies are de-stuffing the family room couch and chasing and being chased by the Shanleys, two cats, Sierra and Ninja (a large Siamese).

True to boxer character he is loyal, gentle, and friendly despite a menacing look.

BARBARA LOUNSBERRY *is the daughter of a political reporter and colum-*
nist. As a 10-year-old, she got to sit in the "Press Box" at the Iowa legis-
lature and in the first row at the Governor's press conferences—thanks to
her father's press credentials. She loved it when the legislature changed
to annual sessions. Now an adult, Barbara is the Nonfiction Editor of
The North American Review, *the oldest literary magazine in the United*
States. She is a professor of English at the University of Northern Iowa
and is the author or editor of four books: The Art of Fact; Contemporary Artists of Nonfiction *(1990);* The Writer in You *(1992);* Writing
Creative Nonfiction: The Literature of Reality, *co-edited with best-*
selling writer Gay Talese (1996), and The Tales We Tell: Perspectives
on the Short Story, *co-edited with Stephen Pett of Iowa State Univer-*
sity, Susan Lohafer of the University of Iowa, and R. C. Feddersen of Okla-
homa (1998).

JOE SHARPNACK *is an Iowa City editorial cartoonist who currently pro-*
duces cartoons under contract for the Iowa City Gazette. *His work has*
appeared in numerous domestic and international publications includ-
ing USA Today, The Washington Post, *and the* Financial Times of
London.

    He is also the drummer for Oink Henderson and The Squealers, the
sensational Iowa based rock & roll trio that is ". . . not responsible for
questionable performances, poor taste or paranormal aberrations at any-
time during the show."

    His play, Little Cheep-Cheep the Chicken *was rejected by New York*
play publishers Samual French, Inc.

AMY ROACH *is a graphic designer at The University of Iowa where she*
has produced award-winning periodicals for the past 14 years. She
graduated with honors from Illinois State University in 1983. Amy lives
in Cedar Rapids with her husband, Jim, and their three children. She
has always been an Independent voter.